Hotdish To Die For

By
Pat Dennis

Penury Press   Minneapolis, MN

0 9 8 7 6 5 3 2

Printed in the United States of America

Cover Photograph by Steve Dennis

Cover Models: Pat Dennis, Marjorie Myers Douglas, Mary Rogers, Zola Thompson

Book design: Wild Thoughts, Minneapolis, MN 612/927-8018

Library of Congress Catalog Number: 99-96219

Dennis, Pat

Hotdish To Die For!
SUMMARY: A collection of culinary mystery short stories including hotdish recipes.

ISBN: 0-9676344-0-7

To Steve

My partner in life

and to

Zola Thompson

Mary Rogers

Marjorie Myers Douglas

My partners in crime

CONTENTS

Introduction

Hotdish Mystery: The Unofficial Guide

Short Stories

Death By Idaho

Cabin Fever

The Elder Hostile

Hotdish To Die For

The Lutheran Who Lusted

The Maltese Tater Tot

Recipes

Hotdish Recipes

Hotdish Mystery:
The Unofficial Guide

Definitions

Hot: 1) marked by a higher temperature; 2) given a sensation of burning.

Dish: 1) a vessel used for serving food; 2) the food served in the dish.

Hotdish: 1) midwestern colloquialism for a hot entree that is similar to a French casserole except that it is often inedible; 2) the bastard offspring of canned Cream of Mushroom soup.

Hotdish Mystery: 1) a culinary mystery short story where a hotdish is somehow involved in a crime; 2) a reiteration of the fact that it is often a crime to serve hotdish.

I do not fully comprehend hotdish, nor should I. Like most baffling compulsions, hotdish addiction is genetic, linked to frugal ancestors who first arrived in the midwest via wagon trains and broken-down Buicks. Those pioneers (who could have chosen to continue west to sunny California or south to balmy Florida) looked around at the often-frozen tundra and the flat treeless prairies of the heartland and said, "Let's live here."

They were the early settlers of Minnesota, Wisconsin, Iowa and the Dakotas. And through the years, besides harsh winters, hungry mosquitoes and a reasonable amount of common sense, the residents of these states shared an obsession - hotdish.

Regional cuisine is not unusual. The eastern seaboard is renowned for its succulent clam chowders. To Southerners, a good gumbo is manna from heaven. And westerners will always salivate over mouth-watering barbecues.

But in the heartland we, and we alone, revere something called hotdish. For those who are not familiar with hotdish (i.e. the rest of the civilized world), it is an entree whose origins are canned soup, canned vegetables, white rice and a scattering of I-got-it-on-sale meat. The dish is then cooked in oven-proof bakeware and served, well, hot.

Not a lot of brain power was used in coming up with the name hotdish.

My work as a comedian and mystery writer has led me to eat hotdish in Lutheran church basements, Catholic universities and at family reunions. I have eaten it in the homes of the poor, wealthy, and intellectually elite. I have discovered that even holding a Ph.D. cannot protect a heartlander from having an uncontrollable urge to serve guests ground hamburger and white rice that is gaily covered with Tater Tots and then drenched in canned, creamed soup and baked until every possible drop of moisture is sucked out.

Perhaps it is because I am originally from Chicago that I find hotdish both amusing and comforting. And perhaps it is because I suffer from what is currently called food issues that I find hotdish frightening.

My dilemma with food began as a child. My parents were relocated southerners. My father was a machinist at Inland Steel in Chicago. My mother was a housewife, devoted both to her fundamental-ist church and to serving me enormous breakfasts of sausage patties, fried eggs, homemade biscuits and red-eye gravy.

My father often worked second shift and there would be my mom and I, alone, glued in front of The Lawrence Welk Show. She'd offer to make the two of us a little something. The little something was usually a plate of homemade walnut fudge, served warmed with butter still melting on top. We'd eat a bit of the fudge and put the rest in the ice box for my father who, unlike my mom and I, was skinny as a rail. Dad would be home at eleven. The fudge never made it past nine.

As a mystery writer it is a natural progression for me to combine my own obsessions into my tales. Food has been, and always will be, an issue with me. At times it has been my best friend and at others my worst enemy. And if you are what you eat, I am my own hotdish. I am fat and comfort-able, a little too salty yet somehow rather bland.

The inspiration for *Hotdish To Die For* came from a women's club luncheon where I was the speaker. The buffet was elaborate with dozens of hotdishes, lime-green Jello molds with tiny marsh-mallows and shredded carrots, and nut-laden chocolate and caramel dessert bars.

As the guest of honor I was asked to be at the head of the line. I stared at the artery clogging horizon that lay ahead of me and thought, "My God, this stuff could kill you."

Welcome to my world.

Death by Idaho

The one thing Lars Tolefson was sure about was his marriage. It was pure and simple. He hated his wife and she hated him.

They had met in the late sixties, a time of turbulence everywhere except, of course, in central Minnesota where tie-dye did not replace flannel and Bobby Vinton was more popular than The Beatles.

Lars met Ingrid at the annual Sons of Norway banquet. She was standing behind the buffet table serving her original hotdish specialty - "Company's Coming Potatoes."

As Ingrid scooped her creation onto Lars' plate, he told her that people in Iowa were uppity because they called hotdishes "casseroles." Ingrid said she'd heard.

"That's why I'm glad I'm from Minnesota," Lars told her. "We ain't got a reason to be snooty."

Before the evening was over, Lars came back for seconds and then thirds. It was the food that attracted him, not Ingrid. He was more interested in a hearty meal than an affair of the heart. But he was almost thirty and decided marriage may not be such a bad thing after all. Besides he had little to give so he had almost nothing to lose.

Ingrid, he decided, would be as good as any woman out there. All females were the same to him - trouble with a capital T. Every woman he had ever known had wanted to change him, make him into some sort of a damn success or something.

But Ingrid seemed like she might be less trouble than most. She was mouselike in nature and would scurry across a room. Lars even half smiled when he saw her nibbling on crackers in the corner.

A mouse of my own, he smirked and began to set the trap.

He liked the fact that Ingrid was shy and plain. He even liked her severe case of adult acne and the fact that he was the first man she ever dated. Lars knew he'd never lose her to anyone else. He thought no one else would want her.

Within two months they were married. They honeymooned at a Motel Six on Highway 61. Lars told Ingrid that the small, musty room was the honeymoon suite. By then, Ingrid knew better than to contradict him.

Later that night Lars pranced around the room, proud as a peacock for losing his virginity in only a matter of seconds. He was so astonished at his own sexuality that he had little interest in Ingrid's.

Ingrid herself became quieter and quieter as the months went by. Lars wouldn't have noticed her except for her odd habit of turning up the volume when Peggy Lee's song "Is That All There Is?" played on the radio.

They had children, of course. Three in all. The eldest they hadn't seen for six years. He joined the army at 18, feeling at home for the first time in his life. He'd call his parents once a year, at the holidays, just to see if they were still alive.

The middle child, Dee, lived in Sioux Falls. She'd grudgingly visit at Christmas, her arms filled with wrapped clearance items. She, too, dashed across the living room like her mother. Her father called her Mini-Mouse. No one ever laughed.

The baby, all four hundred pounds of him, lived in the basement, addicted to television reruns of "Scooby Doo" and bottles of Pig's Eye Beer.

So it was rather easy for Lars to know, as he looked out his living room window on a blustery Minnesota winter afternoon, how pathetic his own life had become. It was just like the filthy, exhaust-covered snow piling high in the gutters in front of his rundown house. Lars was convinced that he, too, had been born pure and white like the powdery flakes that had fallen from the heavens. His only sin was being covered with the crap of others.

As far as Lars could see, there was only one glimmer of hope he could hold on to. And to him, it sparkled like sunlight. He called it "The Plan" and it was time to put it into action.

The Plan, like most plans, was devised to get "The Money" - the $200,000 from Ingrid's life insurance. Lars had been clever enough to make sure there were policies on both of them, not only Ingrid. He knew a single policy on the dearly departed would look too suspicious. He'd watched too many episodes of "Matlock" to make that mistake.

It was the perfect time for the perfect plan for the perfect murder.

It was their thirty-year wedding anniversary. He was sure the tragedy of it all would outweigh any suspicion.

"Thirty years!" he said to himself over and over. It sounded more like a prison sentence than a holy union. As far as he was concerned, he should have been paroled years ago for good behavior.

He'd always been faithful to the mouse, except, of course, for the twelve-year affair with a waitress from New Ulm. But who could blame him? Her breasts were as large as summer melons.

He had been a blameless husband and a wonderful father. He had done his share. It was time to get on with his life before it was too late.

It was Lars who had arranged for the three-room cabin at Pine Point Resort, nestled along the shores of Lake Superior. It was Lars who insisted they celebrate a day that had never before been noted.

He looked at the clock. It was 2:30 p.m. He stood up and put on his green plaid insulated jacket and yanked on his fur-lined orange cap and pulled the flaps down over his ears. He checked himself in the mirror, flexing his flabby biceps in the process. He still had no idea why his youngest called him Elmer Fudd.

He walked into the kitchen and saw Ingrid packing the cardboard food box for their trip up north.

"What's this crap?" Lars said, peering into the box.

"Food," Ingrid answered, emotionless as usual.

"This ain't food, it's hair spray," he said, half-way pulling the can out of the box. "Why is there hair spray mixed in with the kitchen stuff? Are you crazy?"

"There ain't enough room in my purse," she answered, her voice as empty as their marriage.

"Just don't mistake the hair spray for that Pam stuff," he mumbled. He wanted to add "you idiot" but he was trying to be nice. Just because he was going to kill her didn't mean he was going to treat her bad on their last day together.

He picked up the box and then dropped it down angrily. "You dummy. I like potatoes but you're bringing too many. There's gotta be ten pounds of 'taters in here. We're only going for two days!"

"They cook down," she said coldly, and Lars knew there would be no convincing her. The woman was a virtual doormat except when it came to her cooking. If she was determined that they'd eat her damn potato hotdish for two days straight, they'd eat her damn potato hotdish for two days straight.

Then, with relief, Lars saw something else he could complain about. "What's that thing?"

"What thing?" Ingrid asked, zipping up her garage-sale parka.

He reached into the box. "What the hell are you doing with a pink plastic pipe?"

"It's a gourmet rolling pin. I bought it at the Galleria. Cost me $10.00."

Lars picked up the food box and stormed out of the house. Ingrid followed, quiet as ever.

"You spent $10.00 on a damn piece of plastic? You'd better not wonder why we're poor!"

"I don't," Ingrid answered.

She knew why. Lars worked most jobs only a few months before he was fired.

"I just thought it was pretty," she said, scraping ice off the car window. "Sometimes a woman just needs something pretty."

"Humph," Lars responded, his mouth bulging with chewing tobacco. For the entire three-hour ride to Lake Superior, every fifteen minutes or so he'd growl out "money down the drain" and then spit the chewed, dark brown, liquid slime into a tin can he kept on the car floor.

He knew that if he didn't have The Plan, he would demand she repay him the $10.00 on the spot. But The Plan would take care of everything. It would wipe out three decades of misery.

It was twilight when he pulled into the resort's parking lot. Even though Lars was still upset at Ingrid, he knew he had to put on a good face for the clerk,

"Cold enough for ya?" The clerk asked as Lars came through the doors, stomping snow off his boots.

"Could be colder," Lars answered with a tight smile as he picked up a pen to sign the register.

"I got a reservation," Lars said proudly, knowing he'd gotten there before the six o'clock deadline for those guests who didn't have a credit card to secure the cabin.

"Number Nine," the clerk said as he handed Lars a key quaintly attached to a pine cone with the number painted in white.

"It's my weddin' anniversary," Lars announced.

"Congratulations," the clerk said, noticing the dark tobacco stains covering the front of Lars' jacket.

"Yes sir, thirty years today. Love the little woman the same as the day I married her," Lars said, knowing that was not a lie.

Lars got back into the car and drove down the winding short path to their cabin. All of the roads had been plowed. And more importantly, he knew, ahead of time, that the path to the Lighthouse had been cleared. He had called the State Park earlier that day. He was smart enough to use a pre-paid phone card, thanks to wisdom obtained from watching "Homicide" every week.

Split Rock Lighthouse State Park was a popular destination spot for morons like his wife. Ingrid collected lighthouse crap. It was all over their house. Lighthouse pot holders, lighthouse candle sticks, lighthouse switch plates. She'd save for months just to buy a stupid lighthouse-shaped key ring that flashed a light when she used it.

"What do you think you are," Lars would complain. "A friggin' lost ship at sea?"

He'd grown to hate lighthouses so he knew Ingrid was caught off guard when he suggested they spend their anniversary night at the resort near Split Rock. She readily agreed.

The Plan was working. Tonight he would push her over the cliff. Once he was sure she was dead, he'd run to the Ranger Station to report the accident.

It was so foolproof that the moment Lars and Ingrid walked into the cabin he insisted they leave immediately for the State Park.

"Now?" Ingrid asked. "I haven't even made supper."

"Supper can wait," Lars said, thinking that if The Plan worked quick enough he'd be able to enjoy a midnight snack at the Baker's Square he passed on the way.

"We'll make it a quick visit," he grunted as he pulled a pair of *Winter Shoe Studs* out of his pocket. It was a gadget he'd ordered from an ad in TV

Guide, a pair of rubber straps that were covered with pointed metal studs. The straps were guaranteed to "cling to ice" and "prevent falling." Lars had ordered only one set.

"I'm making dinner first," Ingrid said firmly, and Lars knew that was that.

"Hell, you'll stuff me so full of food I won't want to go anywhere," he grumbled and sat down in front of the cabin's black and white television set, pissed off at the world.

At least she was cooking his favorite hotdish, Lars thought. That was the one thing he'd miss.

"They fresh potatoes?" he bellowed from the couch.

"I bought the bag yesterday at Cub, got ten pounds for $1.88. They were running a special. I took it as a sign."

"Humph " he huffed, as if she'd know what a sign was. "Idiot," he said out loud knowing she couldn't hear him over the noise from the television.

Lars settled himself into the lumpy sofa and put his feet up on the coffee table. He didn't even bother to take off his boots with the ice catching points. Lars knew the resort owner expected guests to treat the furniture like they'd treat a rental car - use it and abuse it.

As a Vikings cheerleader paraded across the fuzzy screen, Lars settled into his favorite fantasy of wealth. He knew it would take 30 days or so to get the check from the insurance company and another month or so to sell the house. It would only take a day or two to get his son's fat ass out of the basement. Then Lars, who'd never been farther than the Wisconsin Dells, would move to Costa Rica.

He knew all about Costa Rica from his survival magazines. A man could live like a king in Costa Rica even if he was on Social Security. It would be heaven to be there with his insurance jackpot. He didn't notice that in all of his daydreams, he looked twenty years younger and possessed a personality that was pleasing rather than annoying. And on each arm, clung an awestruck Spanish beauty.

For the last three months he'd taken to carrying a *Speak Spanish in Three Days* booklet in his front pocket. Ingrid had noticed it but never said a word.

"Como esta?" he would say to himself over and over again. "Como esta?"

He closed his eyes and imagined the murder. He had learned about visualization while watching "The Oprah Show."

He visualized leaving the cabin with Ingrid and driving to the State Park entrance. He saw himself telling the Ranger at the gate that it was their anniversary and they wanted to see the stars. He saw the Ranger eating that up. State employees were as big a fools as the federal ones.

He imagined how he and Ingrid would walk up the path to the lighthouse. He actually felt himself take Ingrid's hand. He saw her being so surprised when he touched her that she followed without questioning.

In his mind, he led her to the "You Are Here" sign at the far edge of the cliff. He smiled as he pushed her over. He watched her tumble over the jagged rocks like a giant troll doll headed for hell.

He knew that when the police dragged the body from the lake, she'd still be wearing the wilted corsage he bought that morning. He had insisted, of course, that she pin it tightly on her coat.

And Lars' eyes would be filled with real tears. He had learned from "The Geraldo Rivera Show" that a lot of killers were caught because they never shed tears when questioned about their deceased loved ones. Lars had taken to carrying a bottle of onion juice in his jacket. Unlike every other aspect of his life, The Plan was meticulous. And unlike every other get-rich-quick scheme he'd ever tried, from gambling to chain letters, this one would work.

"Buenos noches," he whispered as he used the remote to switch off the television set. "Buenos noches."

Lars was so immersed in his final visualization exercise that he failed to notice Ingrid standing in the doorway. In one hand she held the plastic pipe she had called a gourmet rolling pin. It was now stuffed with a potato on one end and the other end was capped off. Hair spray had been sprayed through a hole that was drilled in the top of the pipe.

In Ingrid's other hand she held a yellow Bic lighter.

Out of the corner of his eye he saw Ingrid light the opening of the pipe. In the last millisecond of his life, he recognized the scent of Aqua Net and baked potato as it shattered his temple and caused him to fall into the wooden stove, cracking open his head in the process.

Ingrid, too, was shocked that the homemade spud gun she had read about in one of Lars' stupid magazines actually worked. She had known for years that he someday would try to kill her. That fact never really bothered her though. Lars had failed at everything else he had tried in life. She knew he'd fail at that.

"He tripped on one of those silly traction things he put on his boots," she told the police when they arrived.

The Lake Superior Police believed her. They didn't bother with forensics or other such non-sense. They relied on their instincts. They could tell Ingrid had been a devoted wife for 30 years. Even in her grief, she was kind enough to offer the police a hotdish she had been cooking.

It was a shame it had to happen on their thirti-eth anniversary, the police told her.

Yes, she answered, wiping her watery eyes. She had always been allergic to hair spray.

It took only a month for Ingrid to get the insur-ance check and another month to sell the house. It only took a half day to convince her baby boy he had to get out of the basement and into their new car.

Their first stop was a lighthouse in Wisconsin.

Cabin Fever

"I'm selling the lake cabin," Pete Tagney announced to his son as he put on his Minnesota Twins baseball cap and walked to the door of his northeast Minneapolis house.

"You're what?" Jeff asked, looking up for the first time that morning from the television set. Jeff, like a lot of kids, was mesmerized by cartoons. The only difference was that Jeff was thirty-four.

"I'm going to move to Las Vegas. I can't take Minnesota winters anymore. I'm too old."

"But what about me?" Jeff yelled, throwing the remote against the back wall.

"What do you care what the temperature is? You go from the couch to the car to the chair you sit in at work. You don't even notice when it snows. If you did maybe you'd shovel the sidewalk sometime."

"I mean what about me and the cabin? You know I love it up there."

"I'm moving to Vegas."

"You already said that. But you don't have to sell the cabin to move. I'll take care of it for you."

"You can't take care of crap,"

"I love the cabin."

"I need the money," Pete said in a tone that said that was that.

"It'll kill me if you sell it!" Jeff whined hopelessly.

"What happens, happens." Pete told him, not impressed by his son's ludicrous remarks. Who ever died because a cabin was sold?

"You die, you die." Pete laughed, leaving the house whistling and heading towards the nearest bar.

No, you die, Jeff said to himself.

For as long as Jeff Tagney could remember, his weekends had been spent at the family lake cabin. Every dawn he sat on the lakeside deck. He'd drink thick, hot coffee from a chipped Minnesota Vikings mug. He'd smoke one Camel cigarette after another and watch as loons skid across the waves. Occasionally, he'd munch on a stale powdered donut as he lifted his binoculars to survey his world.

He'd watch as the Andersons' lights would come on at exactly 6:00 a.m. He knew Joan would be the first one up. She'd shuffle across the worn black and green linoleum floor. She'd turn on the thirty-year-old avocado-green electric range. The percolator would start brewing any minute. Her husband Ben would stagger out the back door, hung over from the previous night's devotion to vodka and tonic. He'd stumble to the cold, clean water front and pee.

Next door were the Roths. The entire family stayed in bed until noon. One by one they'd wake up and one by one they'd bring chaos to the calm. The family owned six jet skis, four chain saws, one wood chipper, four TVs, three VCRs, and two boom boxes. And, just in case there was a rare moment's lapse of silence, their German shepherd would question loudly as to why.

Fourteen families in all lived on the lake. And, as only long-time lake neighbors could do, Jeff loved and hated everyone of them.

If Jeff had been a poetic man, he would understand it was the beauty of the lake that compelled him to make the three and a half hour journey each weekend. But poet he wasn't. His thought process never elevated beyond the number of fish he caught or how fast the powerboat could go. At thirty-four he was still a kid. And no one loves a cabin at the lake more than a kid.

It was because he loved it so much that Jeff understood what he had to do. He had avoided making too many choices in his life, always afraid he'd make the wrong one. But this time the decision he had to make was obvious even to him. He had to kill his father. And do it soon.

Pete Tagney also liked the cabin. But unlike his son, he also liked other things, such as big-thighed women and all-night gambling.

For forty-five years Pete had been living the Minnesota dream - a good job at the brewery in St. Paul, a mortgage on a solid two-bedroom stucco bungalow in the city and a cabin on a lake.

But at 65 years of age he'd grown tired of winters that were so bad that ice would form on the inside of his car. He was sick of evenings devoted to pulling snow off of his roof with a twenty-foot rake.

He wanted to do what every other proud Minnesotan did - move to a warmer climate as soon as their first Social Security check arrived.

Most of his friends had already moved to Arizona. In the heat of the desert they wore "I Luv Minnesota" t-shirts while they watched for scorpions. In the early evening they'd drive into Sun City, looking for signs of a Polka Band.

Pete Tagney's dream centered on a trailer park outside of Las Vegas. It was a senior community where he could wear Bermuda shorts year round.

He had visited The Lucky View Park the previous year. It was the month after his wife of forty years had died. He had never been to Nevada. An ad in the travel section had caught his eye. Sun Country Airlines was selling a package for $99 that included air and hotel. Until that weekend, Pete had thought the only magical place on earth was the inside of a bass boat.

But the bright lights of Las Vegas bedazzled him more than any Northern star could. The allure of a double wide for under $30,000 and the dozens of well-built and willing women who, at fifty-five, strutted brazenly about the trailer park pool in tiny bikinis, was enough to drive him insane.

His wife had been a good wife and he had loved her but Ethel was always more interested in cooking than in sex. He could count on her for a tasty hotdish but a hotdish herself she wasn't.

All his life Pete had heard of women like the ones he saw at Lucky View. He was sure each was a former show girl. Their breasts, though half a century old, were still firm enough to lay his head on.

He knew he could have every one of them if he wanted to. All he had to do was move there. And to do that he only had to sell the cabin.

Of course his first choice would have been to sell it to his son, Jeff. He'd then be able to come back to the lake whenever he wanted to. He could even bring one of his new girlfriends back with him. But he knew Jeff would never be able to buy the cabin. His son didn't have a dime. As far as his father knew, he never would.

Jeff was aware that his father thought he was little more than a bum. Jeff knew his dad didn't approve of his lifestyle, but Jeff didn't care. He liked his job as a security guard. It not only paid eight bucks an hour but after he punched in, all he had to do was sit. And his salary, up to this point in his life, had covered all his needs. It paid the forty bucks he gave his dad every week for room and board, bought his Mad Magazines, and there were always a few bucks left over for scratch-off lottery tickets and porno video rentals.

Jeff thought his life would always be the same - good enough until his father would die and then it would be great. He would have the cabin all to himself. He might even find a woman or two to bring up to the lake. Owning property was the strongest aphrodisiac.

But now his dad was destroying his life by putting the cabin on the real estate market. His father was giving up Minnesota to relocate to a radioactive dump in the desert. As far as he was concerned, his father had gone insane, like an old dog with rabies that had to be put down.

The cabin was meant to be his. It was his birthright - just like the fact that his eyes were green like his mother's, and his lips thin and cracked like his dad's.

Jeff knew he would die if he lost the cabin, He would do whatever it took to keep it. And he would have to do it now, this weekend, before it was listed in the StarTribune real estate section and hundreds of potential buyers descended on his birthright.

Jeff did not want any damn yuppie from the Twin Cities traipsing through his cabin bedroom, smirking at his Star Wars bedspread and his Babes of Baywatch Calendar.

His dad was planning to go to the real estate office on Monday to sign the papers. He couldn't let that happen. By then Pete Tagney would have drowned and no one at the lake would be surprised. Everyone knew that from time to time Pete Tagney got a little too drunk and drove his speed boat a little too fast.

Jeff wasn't partial to what he had to do. If he had his druthers he'd let his father live. Even though he didn't like him much, he had always seemed to be there. Not there for him, of course, just there.

Things change, Jeff said to himself as he and his father drove up north to the cabin for the weekend. Things change, he said again, as they finally pulled into the cabin's driveway.

As Pete turned off the Ford Escort, Jeff glanced at his watch. It was 8:43 PM. The same time they arrived every Friday. Pete pulled the key out of the ignition and tucked it over the visor.

"I'll get the groceries," Jeff stated, quickly opening his door and grabbing the two bags from the back seat. His father shot him a surprised look and then shrugged his shoulders and headed for the cabin.

Jeff followed. Pete opened the cabin door and walked straight to the television. He began to jiggle with the rabbit ears that sat on top of the set.

"I'll just put away the groceries for now," Jeff said.

"You gonna announce everything you do?" Pete mumbled. He had never seen the kid so talkative. "You going to tell me when you're going to fart, too?"

Jeff tried to laugh.

"Good one, Dad," he said and walked into the kitchen.

Some people deserve to die.

Jeff set the bags down and began to put away the groceries. A box each of Frosted Flakes and Count Chocula, two loaves of white bread, a tub of margarine, generic raisins, rippled potato chips and a ring of bologna.

Neither one of them had eaten well since Ethel died. Jeff was reminded of that every time he opened the kitchen cabinet doors.

Inside were what he called his mother's remains - cans and cans of mushroom soup, envelopes of onion soup mix. a box or two of Uncle Ben's rice mix. He knew that in the back of the freezer was a big bag of Tater Tots.

There was enough oil in one of Ethel's recipes to grease a pig.

He'd often thought about making one of his mother's hotdish recipes. Ethel had typed up all her recipes on 3" x 5" index cards. The card file, covered in brightly flowered contact paper, sat in the center of the kitchen counter.

Jeff strolled from the kitchen. "How about me making Mom's chicken and wild rice dish for dinner tomorrow night?" Jeff said.

"Humph," his father answered. "Damn Duluth. You can never get it. You'd think they would have had invested in a decent transmitter by now."

"A nice big hot meal," Jeff said again.

"Do whatever you want," Pete snapped. Damn kid! Why wasn't he buried in his room like he usually was.

"Okay, so we'll just plan on it then," Jeff said.

"Humph," his father answered.

Jeff went to his room and opened the patched nylon gym bag he carried his clothes in. Inside was his arsenal.

His plan was complicated, but he knew he could carry it off. First, he would make two separate hotdishes for dinner. One for him and one for his dad. Of course the hotdish itself would be the same, but one of the dishes would have an additional touch.

Jeff had purchased five boxes of over-the-counter sleeping pills at Walgreens. He knew the pills themselves wouldn't be enough to kill his dad, but the combination of Jack Daniel's, crushed pills, and a push into the deepest part of the lake would.

Jeff walked back into the front room of the cabin. He decided to spend his dad's last evening with him. Maybe they could even play checkers. They did that one time.

"The station come in yet?" Jeff asked as he fell on the moldy blue Lazy Boy chair that was broken into a permanent fold back position.

"Does it look like it god-damn did?" His dad was still jiggling with the antenna. It always took a good thirty minutes to adjust the set.

Jeff had long ago stopped asking his dad to buy a satellite dish. When the cabin was his he'd get one big enough to get Mars on.

Jeff lit a cigarette and took a long, satisfying puff. There was something oddly comforting in watching his father do the same old thing and yet knowing he'd never have to see him do it again. Jeff flicked an ash into an oversized dented, green metal ashtray that was filled with two weeks worth of ashes.

"Here we go," Pete, huffed watching the picture come into focus. His favorite TV show, *America's Most Wanted*, was about to start. They watched TV together until they both fell asleep in front of it.

By 5:00 p.m. the next day, Pete had mowed the yard, scrubbed the floors, and fixed a torn screen. He was preparing the house for the market. Meanwhile Jeff was preparing their last supper.

Jeff was glad he was more angry at his father than usual. It stopped any doubts he might have had. His dad had criticized and ignored him all day. Every time he could, his dad made a snide remark. Pete told Jeff it was too bad he didn't have a real son, one that would help him do chores instead of spending his morning in the kitchen, like a little girl. His father mumbled that when he finally moved to Las Vegas, at least he'd only have to pick up his own shit.

His father taunted Jeff about the big bucks he would get by selling the cabin. He told his son he might even take a thousand or two and spend a weekend in a luxury suite at Caesar's Palace before he moved into his double wide. He heard the suites had 24 hour dirty movies and a slot machine next to the john. He could hit a jackpot while he took a crap.

Comment by comment, Jeff's rage built inside of him. He had spent nearly 35 years putting up with the old man and all he was going to get from it was a postcard saying "Greetings from Lost Wages."

Jeff pulled the two casseroles out of the oven. They were identical dishes comprised of chicken pieces, a box of Uncle Ben's rice, a can of mushroom soup in each, milk, and onion soup mix sprinkled on top. Only his father's had over-the-counter sleeping pills added to it.

He wasn't stupid enough to accidentally switch the casseroles. To serve it he'd use two different plates - not hard to do since none of the dishes matched anyway. His father's would be chipped white china while his would be green plastic. He would spoon out the servings in the kitchen. His father would be none the wiser.

The hotdish aroma filled the cabin. If nothing else, his mother was a good cook. This dish smelled almost as good as hers.

Jeff picked up the plates and headed to the front room. The two of them always ate in front of the TV. The second part of Jeff's plan was already in full swing. His father was a third of the way through the bottle of Jack Daniel's that he had bought him as a surprise.

And now all Jeff had to do was to make a bet with his father. Pete Tagney accepted every challenge his son ever made to him. He never turned down a chance to humiliate his son. Tonight would be no different.

"How's that Jack?" Jeff asked, watching his father lift the bottle to his mouth. His father never bothered using a glass when he drank.

"You're blocking the TV," Pete replied. "Jerry Springer's on. You know I love that show. I don't know where they get such crazy people from."

"Yeah," Jeff answered, setting his dad's food in front of him on the rickety metal TV tray.

Jeff plopped on the couch next to his dad. He watched as he started to eat the hotdish.

"It's fun watching those drag queens fight," Pete said. "I like that."

Jeff watched as his father ate, drank and yelled at the television. Jeff realized he wouldn't miss his father at all. Not even for one second.

He and his father could be guests on that Jerry's show. The topic would be "Fathers and Sons Who Hate Each Other's Guts."

It was time to set the final part of his plan into action. He waited for a commercial to come on.

"You know, Dad, I think it's good you're moving to Vegas. You are getting really old."

"I still got a few good years left in me."

"I don't know about that. You're moving slower than you used to. Your reflexes ain't what they used to be," Jeff said, smiling as he saw the bottle was already half empty. His father's speech was already slurred.

"I can still kick your ass," his father said, spitting out a mouthful of the casserole. "This hotdish isn't like your mom's."

"No, but it'll do the trick," Jeff smiled. "I noticed we nearly got sideswiped by a semi in

Hinckley."

"That was the semi driver's damn fault, you idiot."

'Well, I was just thinking, maybe you shouldn't drive the boat this weekend. It's a lot to handle and..."

"You think I'm too old to drive a god-damn boat?" Pete yelled, trying to rise up but sinking further into the couch in the process.

"Well, not now. You're drunk as a skunk."

"Get your fat lazy ass up." Pete said, managing to stand. "We're going for a ride. I'll show you who can drive a boat.

"I don't think that's such a good idea," Jeff said. "You can hardly stand much less steer a..."

"You little piece of shit," Pete said heading out the back door.

Jeff followed his father outside.

He had already siphoned gasoline from the boat's tank. The two of them would run out of gas in the middle of the lake. When the boat stopped, his father would turn and look at the motor and then Jeff would push him overboard. He'd be too drunk to fight back.

Jeff stepped into the boat with his father and put on his life jacket. He asked his dad if he wanted to wear one. His father swore at him for making the suggestion. And called him a pussy for wearing one.

Jeff smiled. So far, if he had to undergo a lie detector test, he could honestly swear he had asked his dad not to drive the boat and had asked him to wear a life jacket.

Pete started the boat and pulled out into the lake at full blast. It was late and there were no other boats.

"You're going too fast," Jeff yelled to his dad, noting another warning he could tell the police that he had given his father. They were halfway across when the motor died.

"What the hell?" Pete stood up, barely able to because of the liquor and the sleeping pills.

He turned his back to his son. Jeff leaped in the air and quickly pushed his father overboard. Pete's worn Reebok hit him in his chin as he went sailing into the deep.

Pete went under once and then came up again. Even in the darkness Jeff could see how surprised his father was. Jeff leaned over the side and reached his hand to his father. As soon as his father tried to grab it, Jeff pulled his hand away.

"I reached my hand out to my Dad," he would tell the cops.

Pete only went down one more time. Jeff waited a few minutes before he started yelling for his father. Cabin lights turned on across the lake. He knew a dozen eyes and ears were now focused on him. He stripped off his life jacket in order to swim better and jumped into the water.

It was cold but Jeff knew he would survive. In a few minutes other boats would arrive to help him and his father. Only he alone would know that his father would be, by that time, at the bottom of the lake, or so he thought. Jeff had always been impatient. Once again he had not waited long enough. As he hit the water his father came up one more time.

"Son?" his father gasped.

"Dad?" his son answered. It was one of the nicest interchanges they'd ever had.

Pete Tagney grabbed onto his son's belt and they both headed downward. It wasn't until the next morning that police divers found their bodies.

"We're not surprised," Mr. Anderson told the news crew from KDLH that had shown up. "They were a couple of drunks."

"The kid drank more than his old man," Mrs. Anderson added. "He'd down ten beers in an evening and deny he had any."

"Too bad it happened," Mrs. Roth told the media, "that kid loved the lake, more than any-thing."

The Elder Hostile

JP England eased himself up from his manual 1937 Royal typewriter. He had just finished writing his weekly column, "The Elder Hostile." He checked his final sentence and felt pleased with it. It was as nasty as ever.

Slowly he shuffled to the microwave and put a single serving plastic bowl containing a homemade casserole inside. Someone had left the hotdish anonymously outside his apartment door. A note attached read "For JP only. Enjoy!"

"Just another old broad trying to trap me!" he muttered to himself. He had successfully avoided marriage and women for eighty-one years. He was not about to be suckered in now.

JP was, of course, *that* JP England — the infamous curmudgeon and social critic. His column had been, at one time, a national treasure. Now it was reduced to the bottom corner of a four-page newsletter printed by the Senior Association of his apartment complex.

At age 81, the majority of JP's friends had died. His enemies, however, were, as always, multiplying daily. The weekly finger-pointing in his column assured a continuous supply.

The newsletter's editor, Mike Topich, encouraged JP's diatribes. For sixty years Mike had been JP's best, and sometimes only friend. When the editor moved into the senior village, he coerced JP to follow suit.

Mike told JP that the newsletter needed him. He explained that too many of the residents were, like most seniors, afraid to state their views. He knew that JP's natural antagonism was what the residents needed.

"If you're still complaining, you're still alive," the editor had been known to say.

And JP England, if nothing else, was certainly alive. He criticized everyone and everything from the cafeteria chef to the management. He lambasted local government for ignoring the seniors and the federal government for being too intrusive. He wrote eloquent diatribes on the greed of pharmaceutical companies and attacked every senior at the home for being too cheap to give to charity.

"Take some of those bingo bucks you hoard and give it to a bell ringer, for God's sake," was the opening sentence in his last column.

In his sixty years of writing, JP never retracted a word, even if it put his life in jeopardy or made him a target for another slander lawsuit. He took full responsibility for his butchering barbs. He knew he was hated because he despised almost everything and was proud of it.

Of course, there were many things he loved: Mozart, Edward Hopper, and George and Ira Gershwin. There were also lesser erudite fancies such as The Minnesota State Fair, Johnny Cash, The Andy Griffith Show, hotdish and Rex Stout.

Didn't that prove he was human after all? That he wasn't merely an elitist snob?

Still, his readers concentrated on the things he hated. And, unfortunately, his hate list grew daily.

It included any musical by Andrew Lloyd Weber, any movie starring Barbra Streisand after

"Funny Girl," any rock group after the Drifters, Republicans and Democrats as well as any third-party candidates. He abhorred any book of fiction published between 1981 and 1994. He also hated, of course, most television, including PBS, most radio including talk, and almost every movie, including the talkies.

His checkered career of vicious insights and daring accusations had brought down mob bosses, philandering politicians, corrupt movie moguls, greedy tycoons, and the average Joe or Jane who had regrettably come in contact with him on any given day.

So it was no small surprise that when JP placed the hotdish in the microwave it took only thirty seconds before the explosion. The inside of the microwave was covered in gun powder, tuna flakes, sweet peas and cream of mushroom soup.

"Again?" he asked as he looked at the mess. In his 50 year career as a paid curmudgeon, JP had endured at least a dozen attempts on his life. He quickly telephoned the newsletter editor.

Mike showed up within minutes and chuckled as he watched JP scrub the counter. "Any idea who sent it?"

"It could have been any one of a hundred people, although I think most of the likely ones may be dead by now," JP replied as he continued scrubbing.

"Is it column related? If it is, we probably should let the management know about this."

"Don't tell those nosy busybodies a thing! Besides, it's just a prank."

"You could have been hurt."

"I may be older than you, but I think I can survive a few flying noodles."

"Still, I think we should let someone know about..."

"No. If you do, they'll probably shut down the newsletter. Just give me a day or two. I'll figure it out."

"Do you need my help?"

"Of course."

For the next three hours, JP and the editor poured over a year's worth of columns. They decided to go with the odds, knowing that anyone who carried a grudge longer than that had probably died of stress.

"Let's see," Mike said, tallying up his notes, "your five most vicious columns...."

"I prefer the term 'brutally honest'."

"All right. Five of the more brutally honest columns concerned the weekly bingo sessions..."

"I loathe the bingo games. Seventy-five zombies sitting there marking off numbers with a hot pink marker, surrounded by useless good luck charms of plastic, blue-haired trolls and green, styrofoam four-leaf clovers. If management is going to allow gambling, at least let it be craps, for God's sake."

"There are the eight columns attacking the ineptness of the cafeteria staff," Mike continued, not paying the slightest attention to JP's ranting.

"Anyone who considers ketchup a vegetable should be tarred and feathered."

"You did eleven exposes on the apartment

management."

"You know as well as I do that if management gave one iota about anything in the newsletter, they'd have shut us down a long time ago. I don't think they even read it."

"And then there's the recent columns about the laundry room thief. Actually, even I thought that was going overboard."

"Overboard! About theft? Just where does the line begin? If one sock is okay to steal then is it all right to steal twenty? Thirty? Five thousand?"

"No one stole anything. Missing socks are an unexplained universal phenomena - like the Bermuda triangle."

"Missing socks, Mike, are the karma of fools. I have never misplaced a thing until I came to this place and then suddenly my socks are gone. My favorite Gold Toe argyles."

"You do realize you are getting older?"

"Which means to me that I am getting wiser. I'll lay you ten to one odds that the laundry room thief is responsible for my exploding lunch."

"That's insane. Even if someone did steal your socks, which to begin with I doubt ever happened, it's a far cry to rigging your hotdish with explosives."

"Anyone who steals will also do anything else - given the reason to do so."

"Do you have a plan on how to catch this phantom thief?"

"Of course."

Within minutes, JP and Mike were knocking on residents' doors. Mike interviewed the residents on the left-hand side of the hallway while JP talked to those on the right side.

"Would you like tea, JP? I have a lovely jasmine." Annie Berkley smiled at JP as he entered her apartment. "I still have a few Pepperidge Farm cookies. They were a gift from my darling niece Laura. She is ..."

"I'm not here to socialize, Mrs. Berkley."

"Miss," Annie giggled at the famous reporter. "My husband ran off with his file clerk twenty years ago. I hear they live in a trailer park outside of Chicago."

"Have you lost anything while doing laundry? Socks, shirts, maybe underwear?"

"Why JP!" Annie said shocked and then blushed. She carefully crossed her support hose covered legs. She did manage, however, to hike her flowered house dress up a few inches in the process.

"For God's sake, Mrs. Berkley," JP said, flustered. "I didn't come here to pry into your underwear. There's been trouble and I think it's related to missing items, starting with those from the laundry room."

"Well, I have lost a few things in the laundry room. I just thought it was, you know, the Sock God."

"The Sock God?" he moaned. "Why do people have all these ridiculous myths about missing socks?"

"How else do you explain it? It's like life - you don't really know what's going on but you've got to come up with some sort of an answer that you can live with. I can live with the concept of a Sock God."

"Mrs. Berkley, I am not here to have a sophomoric discourse on the philosophy of life. Just tell me what was missing."

"A pair of panty hose and one sock."

"Anything else?"

Suddenly, JP noticed Mrs. Berkley's head begin to droop. She transformed herself from a vivacious 70-year-old coquette to a tired, old woman.

After a few moments she looked up and said "It's not laundry I'm missing. I've misplaced my diamond watch. I thought I was getting senile."

By the end of the day, 27 residents confessed to missing or lost items. They also admitted they hadn't told anyone about it. They, too, were afraid they were either going senile or worse - afraid of revenge from the thief.

"What an evil person to steal from little old ladies," Mike told JP over a cup of Sanka in JP's apartment.

"It must be an employee. I doubt if it's another resident. Naturally, the first person who comes to mind is James."

"The security guard?"

"He's the most obvious because he has passkeys. Then there's the maintenance man, Thomas. Of course, it could be that dreadful air head activity director."

"Tiffany?"

"Why would anyone in her right mind think that the elderly want to sit around gluing glitter on paper plates? Does she think we're children?"

"That doesn't make her a thief."

"No, but it makes her stupid and stupid people do stupid things, like stealing stupidly."

"Anyone else?"

"Nurse Wretched, or as I called her in one of my columns, Phyllis Wretched. You'd think someone in the medical profession would at least pretend to like people. I think she's a nurse because she gets to jab a hundred people a day."

"You wrote that in one of your columns."

"I did?" JP asked and then smiled. "Well, it's no wonder I have a reputation."

JP moved to his computer and began a file on the persons he now considered suspects. Mike reminded him that he was jumping to conclusions in assuming that the thief and the explosives expert were one and the same.

JP reminded Mike that jumping to such conclusions had served him well most of his life. He was sure his ability to quickly assess a sticky situation would triumph once again. He wanted to catch the thief now more than ever. To send he, himself, a tainted lunch was one thing, but to invade the homes of his neighbors was quite another.

Within the hour he was walking to the activity room.

"JP England!" Tiffany squealed as he entered the room. "I never thought I'd see the day when you joined us! Please sit down!"

The group of female residents seated around the table stared at JP. He couldn't tell if they were afraid or in shock. There were enough open mouths to train a school of dentists.

"We're making decoupage frames today! And it's so easy that even you can do it." Tiffany did not catch the look of disgust that JP sent her way.

"Would you like paper rose cutouts or paper daisies?" she asked him gaily.

"Daisies," he heard himself saying to the delight of three chortling women.

For two hours JP sat, decoupaging frames and listening to nonstop talk. He endured tales of precocious grandchildren, vicious daughters-in-law, perfect sons and a half-hour discussion of a local radio personality Joe somebody whom he reminded them of.

The women described how Joe's primarily male audience tuned in to the show from radios hidden in their garages.

JP envisioned a group of pathetic men, alone in their garages, seated in fishing boats that rested on concrete blocks, drinking cheap beer. Their only possible escape route was down a concrete driveway that was permanently blocked by their wives' expensive cars, the same not-yet-paid-for Detroit-designed barriers that their spouses expected hand waxed every Saturday morning.

The men knew there was no way out. And like noble and valiant prisoners of war, they accepted their entrapment. JP, seated at the arts and crafts table, knew he felt the same existential horror that each of Joe's listeners must have felt. There was nothing more terrifying to a free man than domestic captivity.

By the time JP left the activity room, drained

by useless chatter, he realized Tiffany could not possibly be involved in any crime. There wasn't a vicious bone in her body. If there were, she would not have been able to put up with the endless prattle of her senior students.

JP headed towards the security guard desk, dropping his decoupage frame into the hallway waste can along the way. As usual James was not at his post. James spent most of his days roaming the hallways or snacking in the apartment doorways of women who were still not used to not feeding someone other than themselves.

JP sat at James' desk. He noticed a security camera in the upper hallway corner. Five monitors at the desk showed each of the five hallways in the building. JP also noticed that in the center of the desk was the monitor that JP most often watched - a portable TV that was always turned to a sporting event.

The security guard was a likable fellow. JP found himself losing his reporter detachment and hoped it wasn't him. He glanced around once more, and began opening the security desk drawers. James never bothered to lock anything.

In the center drawer were three packs of Spearmint chewing gum, a box of paper clips, three felt tip markers and a blank "To Do" pad.

In the top side drawer were old issues of *People Magazine* and *National Enquirer*. On the bottom was a three-year-old *Playboy* magazine. JP noticed the subscription label. It had been sent to Elroy Anderson, his 92-year-old neighbor.

In the bottom drawer was a battered thermos,

boots, and a small maroon velvet box. Inside the box was a 14k gold necklace with a tiny ruby pendant. JP closed the drawer just as James arrived.

"Hey, JP how's tricks?" James asked, not caring that JP was seated at his desk.

"Same old, same old," JP smiled at him. He always liked the way James treated him - like he didn't notice his age.

"Did you see the game on Sunday?"

"Great game," JP said, getting up to leave.

"Hey, if you like sitting there, you don't have to get up. I've got to check the second floor anyway."

"Thank you, James," JP said as he watched the security guard saunter down the hallway.

Three hours later, seated in Mike's apartment, JP found himself catching a Heineken that Mike threw his way.

"Who's the next suspect?" Mike asked.

"Nurse Wretched," JP answered.

"Are you going to fake illness?"

"Do you think she'd see me otherwise?"

"Not hardly," Mike laughed, opening a chilled bottle for himself. "At least finish your brew first."

"I wouldn't think of doing otherwise," JP answered.

The nursing station closed everyday at 5:00 p.m. sharp. JP made it by 4:47. The look he received told him that no matter what his ailment was it would be taken care of in thirteen minutes or he would have to come back tomorrow.

"What do you want, Mr. England?" Nurse Wretched asked, not even bothering to look up from her crossword puzzle.

"I'm feeling a little tired lately."

Even with her head down, JP could tell that she rolled her eyes in disgust.

"I think that might be natural at your age."

"True, but I was wondering if there was something you could give me, something to get me going."

The nurse gave him a cold stare and then said, "Do you need energy to write one of your little columns?"

JP understood the insult. He could hardly blame her, knowing he had done five columns in the past year on the nursing department.

"Just a few pep pills would help."

The nurse glanced at the clock. He had already taken up four minutes of her time.

"Wait here," she said as she went into the back room. He heard the cabinet doors being unlocked. He quickly tried to open the drawers of the desk. They were locked, along with everything else in the room. The nurse had padlocks on everything, even the coat closet.

"I appreciate you're doing this," JP said as he swallowed the pills. "I know you rush out every day at five."

"I don't rush, Mr. England, I leave at five. I also arrive every day at eight - not a minute late or a minute early. I have always followed rules."

"Yes, I'm sure. My, you certainly have a lot of locks," he said, looking around the room at all the padlocks on cabinets and drawers.

"There are drugs here, Mr. England and I am the one who is in charge. You have to leave now, even though I am staying later than usual. I'm riding on the residents' bus to Treasure Island Casino."

"As a chaperone?" he asked, surprised she would volunteer for anything.

"I'm just catching a ride. The casino's fifty miles away. My van's been sitting broken in the parking lot for three weeks now. It's a shame this place doesn't pay me a decent salary."

"Yes, it is," JP answered and went to his apartment to call Mike.

Mike laughed as JP relayed his experience at the nursing station. "You actually had the guts to swallow the pills she gave you?"

"I'm sure they were just sugar pills she keeps on hand for raging old coots like me."

"Did you discover anything."

"A little something," JP told him, without going any further.

"Who's next?" Mike asked.

"I think my garbage disposal isn't working properly," JP answered.

A few minutes later JP told the maintenance man Thomas that "the disposal makes a terrible grinding noise."

The maintenance man looked at JP and then said in a voice that sounded as if he were talking to a three-year-old, "A garbage disposal grinds things up. It's supposed to make a lot of noise."

JP wanted to say, "I know that, you idiot" but instead said, "I think it's making more noise than normal. Just check it out. I'll be in the living room watching television."

"Sure thing," Thomas answered and turned on the faucet.

Originally JP had planned to drop a watch into the disposal. He wanted to see if Thomas would return it. But there was a good chance he would wreck both the watch and the disposal. Instead, he did a more sensible thing. He marked a twenty dollar bill with a small red dot in the corner and put it in the silverware drawer next to the disposal.

When he went into the living room, he turned the television volume up to give Thomas a sense of security. It took Thomas only ten minutes to finish.

"I'll be darned if I can find anything wrong with the disposal, though I did replace a washer on your faucet. If the noise starts happening again, call me immediately."

"Sounds good," JP said to him and walked him to the door. As soon as the maintenance man left JP pulled open the silverware drawer. He was not surprised that the money was not there.

It took another half hour for Mike to drop by and comfort the still shaken JP.

"How close were you to calling the police?" Mike asked.

"Too close," JP answered. "I thought I had him dead center."

"And then you found the money on your dresser?"

"I never even put the twenty dollar bill in the kitchen. I had just planned to. You know, for the first time, I think I might be getting old. Maybe I did lose my socks after all."

"Is Thomas off the hook?"

"I think so," JP said, taking another gulp of Heineken, wondering if being in one's eighties actually made him old.

"What about James?"

"Oh, I thought maybe it was him briefly and then I remembered that his girlfriend's name is Ruby. I found a receipt for the jewelry in his top drawer. He paid $125.00 at Sears.

"That's a lot on his salary."

"A man in love," JP said, as if the stupidity of that act explained everything. "Besides, I'm pretty sure I know who our culprit is anyway."

"When will you let me know?"

"Tonight, after the casino bus returns from Treasure Island Casino."

The bus, which ran daily trips to and from the casino, dropped off the last passengers at 10:47 PM. Waiting in the parking lot, behind a parked car with binoculars in hand, were JP, Mike, and the security guard, James.

They watched as the residents filed off the bus. A few managed to smile but JP could tell that most were disappointed. Once again they lost a good portion of their social security checks.

"They should ban that damn bus," JP whispered. "That will be the subject of my next column."

"There she is," Mike said. Nurse Wretched was the last one to get off the bus.

The three waited patiently. Nurse Wretched walked slowly to the bus stop and sat down. Ten minutes later, she looked around to see if anyone was watching and then walked to her van. She opened the door and got in.

"You were right," James told JP. "She is living in her van in the parking lot. I don't understand it. She makes more than I do."

"But you're not a compulsive gambler like she is. She'll never be able to earn enough," JP explained.

"It's gotta be against the rules to live in the parking lot," James said.

"I'm sure it is," JP answered, "but that's not the problem. She's stealing to support her gambling habit. I doubt if she can even afford a roll of toilet paper. Do you have the keys to her office closets?"

"Sure."

"Then let's call the director and get this over with."

By 7:54 a.m. the next morning, when Nurse Wretched stepped out of her van, two policemen were waiting to arrest her. They also had a search warrant. They had found a portion of the missing items in her office. They expected to find the rest in her van.

JP sat at his Royal typewriter, pounding away. His new column was devoted to the ills of gambling. He knew it was one of his better pieces, one that he might even send into *The Pioneer Press*.

Pleased with his detective work, JP didn't even notice that another hotdish had been left in his doorway.

Hotdish To Die For

Every Tuesday morning for the last thirty years, regardless of weather, politics, or interest, the Ripley Book and Chat Society convened at the back table of Neilson's Cafe.

With its blue checkered curtains and mounds of Rice Krispie bars on the counter, Neilson's was, the news editor would later write, an odd place to decide to commit murder.

It was the last week of February and Neilson's top waitress Betty was not in a good mood. Her arthritis was acting up. By eight a.m. she had already shoveled her driveway, carried in a load of logs for her wood furnace, asked her neighbor to jump start her '86 Buick Skylark, and drove two miles down ice-covered streets to work. According to Betty, being single and sixty-one in Minnesota was hell.

Betty had never married. She had only loved once in her life. They courted for two years before he deserted her for someone else. The someone else was the sort of woman who pushed and plotted until she made him a success, though, as far as Betty knew, he never smiled again.

But what was getting to Betty at the moment was not her tragic past, as she referred to it, but "the nut cases" who were waiting to be served at the back table. The Ripley Book and Chat Society.

"Here you go," Betty said through tightened cracked lips as she placed a thermos of coffee on the table.

She already knew what her tip would be. The

total bill would hover around thirty dollars, yet she would receive the usual - one dollar and thirty-seven cents, piled in a mound of pennies, nickels, dimes and the occasional quarter.

The restaurant owner would not let Betty voice her complaint to the women. The leader of the club was married to the most powerful and vindictive man in the county.

"Thanks, Sweetie," Myra Guffman sang gaily, oblivious to Betty's angry feelings. Myra had decided long ago that there were too many people in the world to worry about how they all felt.

Myra had been born the oldest child in a family of fourteen. Her parents worked full-time and Myra, even as a little girl, was left in charge. Now, in her later years, she could see no reason to relinquish her position of authority.

And even though she had never finished reading a complete book in her life, and had no intention of doing so, Myra became the president of the Book Club. Year after year Myra was voted in as president. She enjoyed the position so much, that no one bothered to run against her. Besides, Myra did not need anyone's help. She didn't mind one iota that she did all the work while the others enjoyed a nice breakfast.

Myra's greatest accomplishment to date, besides rising from poverty to becoming the richest women in town, was managing to complete twenty years of psychotherapy without achieving a shred of personal insight.

She had originally gone to therapy to appease her husband's ridiculous assertion that she was too controlling. Myra had, of course, heard that from other people in her life. She was amazed that so many people could make the same mistake. She was not controlling at all. She was only looking out for their best interests.

Originally, Myra had planned to go to only one counseling session. But unfortunately for Myra, it was the 1980's, and the therapist was as greedy and self-centered as the rest of society. His favorite book was "Winning Through Intimidation."

The therapist taught Myra to do daily affirmations such as "I've got to take care of myself first" and "I am wonderful and very, very special." These ego reinforcing declarations gave Myra the internal go ahead to live her life as she always had, without having to notice that she ran over those she cared about in the process.

And by offering to be of service to the Book Club, she easily controlled it. She sent birthday cards to each member. On the first Sunday of the month she'd photocopy the *Star Tribune* Bestseller List and distribute it. She coerced the local weekly shopper, "The Budgeteer," to print, free-of-charge, the time and place of their next meeting, along with an invitation for anyone interested to attend.

But it was this morning's surprising proposal that secured Myra the title "President For Life." It was a single idea that would make everyone in the Society famous - or at least in Ripley's definition of fame - being known in the next county.

"Why read a book when you can write one instead?" Myra asked.

"Are you kidding?" a member asked.

"Write a book? Us?" another laughed.

"Not a real book like...." Myra paused, unable to think of any title.

"Who reads serious books anymore anyway?" she continued. "I think we should write a cookbook. *The Ripley Book and Chat Society's Guide to Hotdish.*"

A collective sigh floated down Main Street. Anything having to do with hotdish would be blessed. It always was.

There was only one fly in the ointment, one light bulb missing, one needle short of a sewing box that morning.

The Visitor.

The unwelcomed appearance of a visitor happened once every few years. It was always someone new to town who had read the invitation in the local shopper and, for some odd reason, believed it meant what it said, that everyone was invited.

There were always problems with visitors. This Visitor was no different. She was still single at forty, had short hair like a man's, was neither a Lutheran nor a Catholic and had the audacity to be from, of all places, Chicago.

A shiver of distrust encircled the room as The Visitor raised her hand.

"What's a hotdish?" she asked innocently.

Of course, because she was from Chicago and not related to a Rotarian or a Swede, Myra reported to her husband later that she yelled in a booming, nasal voice, "What the hell is a hotdish?"

Embarrassed giggles and booming whispers of "here we go again" echoed throughout the room.

They had dealt with drop-ins before. Actual membership came only through a veiled inheritance like a bad habit passed from mother to daughter.

Visitors eventually stopped attending meetings and the Society members were always happy when they did. They were especially glad when the pesky ones stopping coming, those intellectual irritants who thought a book group should discuss books and not the latest town gossip.

This one was, the group could tell, the worst kind of visitor. The type that loves to read. The pasty kind who hide a flashlight under a blanket into the wee hours of the morning, the kind who underline passages and make notes in margins, the kind who would even read the same book twice!

The Ripley Book and Chat Society concluded that real readers were nothing but trouble. And this one, Myra decided the moment she walked through the door, was no different. She had actually been carrying the latest "Oprah Book Club" selection under her arm.

"Don't tell me they don't have hotdish in Chicago?" Myra asked incredulously, her bulbous arms spreading across the table like an obese vulture poised for flight.

"I don't think so," The Visitor said quietly while sinking further into her chair, her face reddening with embarrassment (it was later reported that she stood up and screamed, "Don't question me, you bitch!").

"Well then," Myra answered, flustered at The Visitor's ignorance, "a hotdish is, why, heaven...."

"On earth..." Joan Anderson, the Mayor's wife

continued.

"Or at least in a church basement..." Millie, the church secretary giggled.

"It's potatoes or rice..." Myra added.

"Ground beef and spices," contributed Evelyn, the school bus driver.

And in a rising crescendo Joan added, "Cream of Mushroom Soup."

And then Myra opened her mouth to speak as the others waited breathlessly, knowing by the look on her wrinkled and beaming face, what the final words would be....

"Tater Tots," Myra stated, exclamation point not needed. The two words said it all.

"Oh, you mean a casserole," The Visitor said.

Myra turned, her blues eyes frosty.

"Some call it that," she answered tersely, her voice the temperature of an ice fisherman's butt in January. "In Minnesota it's referred to as hotdish."

"Why?" The Visitor asked.

"Why?" Myra repeated sarcastically, her pretense at politeness evaporating. "Because the dish is served hot, that's why."

"Oh," The Visitor said, with downcast eyes and trembling voice. (That same mumble was later reported to the police as "Die, Bitch, die').

"If there are no further interruptions, I'd like to get on with the meeting," Myra said, managing to smile through clenched teeth.

The meeting continued for hours. They planned the cookbook, they discussed the large photo of the group that would be on the cover and the even larger photo of Myra on the back. Each member agreed to contribute five recipes.

The only minor sign of distress came from Margory Thompson who feared that if the book became popular there would be a dangerous Tater Tot shortage.

But most were happy and upbeat that morning, bathing in the possibility of fame. Myra felt magnanimous and even suggested The Visitor could contribute a recipe. Myra also decided that the book would be completed by the end of April.

There was much to be done, she advised.

The photographs would be taken at Sears. Zola offered a coupon she had been saving for her grandchild's graduation.

The recipes would be typed by Millie. She could easily use the church copy machine without anyone finding out. Praise the Lord for that, she giggled.

The editing would lie with Myra who would have the final decision on any recipe. She reminded everyone that Green Bean Hotdish (topped with seasoned onion rings) was her own personal creation.

Everyone was happy and bouncing around like teenagers forming a garage band. No one, they agreed, could make a meeting more exciting than Myra. And nothing could match Myra's latest vision, they thought, until The Visitor performed an unexpected act.

She made a suggestion. And a good one. One that even Myra could not ignore.

Myra was furious. She was the one who made all the good suggestions for the group. Not anyone else.

"Why not have a Hotdish Festival to celebrate the book's publication?" The Visitor asked.

"What a wonderful idea," Joan blurted out before she realized the idea had not come from Myra.

"It'll be just like the Twin Cities," Mrs. Thompson giggled. "They have a festival every weekend."

"People will come from miles around," Millie chattered.

"Perhaps we can hire a Polka Band," April added.

"Polka and hotdish!" Betty the waitress said in amazement as she refilled the thermos on the table. Even she had gotten in to the swing of things, immediately remembering her own original hotdish recipe. Finally, after all these years of not being noticed, Betty was sure that fame would be hers.

The group hadn't, of course, asked Betty to contribute, but she was sure they would let her. For over thirty years she had given them good ser-vice and in return recieved a pittance. Her Spicy Fisherman's Hotdish must be included in the book.

The excitement was so contagious that even the farmers sitting a table over were tossing out suggestions - "Have a pig race!" "Don't forget the bingo tent!" "There's nothing classier than a tractor pull."

The atmosphere was so charged that it took minutes before anyone noticed that Myra was not joining in the frivolity.

Her arms were crossed tightly in front of her. Her body was tense. Everyone, except Myra, had failed to notice that the idea of the festival wasn't hers.

A disturbing silence fell over the restaurant.

Slowly a few mutterings could be heard. "Maybe a festival isn't such a good idea." "It would be too much work." "Why take the emphasis off the cookbook?"

Myra managed to look each and every person in the eye while avoiding those of Mary, The Visitor. Finally, she spoke.

"The idea of a festival is good," she decreed.

Later, three people testified that at that moment they heard angels singing *The Hallelujah Chorus*. Unfortunately, it was only Jim Nabors on the jukebox.

The first of May would be a good day for a festival, Myra decided. And so it was. Seven hundred people attended the festival, held at the fairgrounds, that sunny day. But only one of them would die.

Five hundred copies of *"The Ripley Book and Chat Society's Guide to Hotdish"* sat in boxes underneath a picnic table. Myra had autographed each one.

The table was placed in the center of the fairway, next to the stage where the Polka Meisters were to perform.

Even Mary, who had now become a member, was there. She had not only contributed her recipe - a daring combination that used not one but four cans of creamed soup - but had designed the cover as well. Her upbeat and positive personality was a bit disconcerting for the other members but they tried to get along with her. Besides, she didn't go away like the others. At least not yet.

The Society members fluttered around the table, each in their Sunday best, high heels sinking into the earth. Myra had ordered corsages for each of the women to wear so they could be easily identified by anyone at the festival. Each member was to carry a basket of books and walk the grounds selling the books person to person, like a group of deranged Amway distributors.

Myra wanted every book sold by the end of the day. She was convinced that the need for a second printing would make headline news for the Society.

Everything was perfect. The big event of the morning was to be a Hotdish Contest. Myra reminded everyone again that the contest was her idea.

She would be the judge. She had even graciously refused to enter her own hotdish though it would, more than likely, be the best.

The contest was to start at 10:00 a.m. It was 9:45 when the crowds began to assemble.

Millie bustled around the table, checking that each hotdish was covered and making sure that the two-hundred feet of extension cords were still plugged in to the fairgrounds' office.

There were to be ten dishes in all (though later the police realized there were eleven). Some were in crock pots, others in Corningware bowls placed on hot trays, a few in Pyrex dishes dressed in homemade cozies. The aroma was more tantalizing than the smell from the mini-donut trailer where circles of batter were bubbling away in hot oil and powdered sugar was dancing in the air.

All ten women lined up behind the table. They were competing for the Grand Prize, a crystal wine goblet engraved with both The Society's and Myra's names.

The hotdishes were placed in random order. No one knew whose hotdish was whose.

Myra stepped up to the table and a silence fell over the crowd. She walked slowly down the row, taking a single bite of each hotdish and then rinsing her mouth with water. She made notes on a little pad she carried. She was stretching the moment as long as she could. Finally, at the end of the line, she made her last scribble.

She lifted her hand to quiet the crowd and began, "Ladies and Gentlemen, it is my pleasure to...."

And then Myra fell forward, collapsing on the table, as a dozen Tater Tots bounced six feet into the air.

Seven hours later, after Myra was declared officially dead by poison, the Society Members were incarcerated at the county jail.

They were still dressed in their Sunday best as they sobbed into handkerchiefs and sheets of toilet paper.

One by one the Sheriff took each of them into the investigation room. The Lutheran church secretary was the first to be interrogated.

"As Jesus is my witness, I loved Myra," Millie swore. For the first time in her life, she understood how easy it was to lie while using the name of her Lord and master.

Later, Margory told the Sheriff, her fingers crossed behind her back, "Myra was kind and compassionate and everyone loved her." She was proud of herself for not laughing out loud. She knew very few people loved Myra.

The newest member, Mary, was the last to be interrogated.

"She was the most controlling woman I've ever known," Mary told the police. "She thought no one could do anything except herself. I didn't like her. I don't think anyone did."

Even the sheriff had to agree.

Mary was returned to the holding cell where Millie was leading the group in "Nearer My God to Thee." Mary just rolled her eyes, wondering why she had stayed with the group, realizing how misled she had been in believing she could actually get the Society to start reading books again.

At the end of the song, no one spoke. The ladies just looked at each other - each trying to figure out who the murderer was. Each one managing to feel guilty that Myra had died and yet surprised that no one felt all that bad.

It was midnight when the sheriff came in and told them all to go home. The killer had been caught. Shouts of "Praise the Lord" filled the room. (This in itself was highly unusual behavior for Lutherans who would rather leave a note on the door than confront anyone in person).

Mary was the one who thought to ask who the murderer was. The sheriff didn't bother to answer as Betty was marched by the cell, still wearing her black uniform, her hands handcuffed behind her while a cigarette dangled from her mouth.

""But why her?" Mary asked.

"I knew it had to be her!" Zola stated even though the name of Betty had never crossed her mind.

"She was angry because we refused to publish her recipe," Margory stated, remembering the awful hotdish Betty would bring every year to the church picnic. "Or do you think she's still carrying a grudge about Wally?"

"Wally?" Mary asked.

"Myra's husband. He and Betty were once engaged, but that was decades ago. Besides, he turned into such a miserable old coot you'd think she'd be happy he left her."

"This is so sad, " Mary sighed as she picked up her purse to leave. "Myra's dead and poor Betty is arrested! Maybe she can claim temporary insanity."

Everyone agreed.

"Does she have anyone to put up bail for her?" Mary asked.

"No," the sheriff answered.

And even though Betty had killed their leader, they - like the good liberal Minnesotans they were - decided to show compassion and contribute to her bail. The group opened their hearts and pocketbooks and put the collected money on the bailiff's table.

"At least it's a start," Millie said as the group walked out of the jail.

The bailiff just stared at the $1.37 in front of him.

The Lutheran Who Lusted

Jenny Borgson, wife and church member, knew she was a good woman. She could always be counted on in emergencies, such as the flooding of the Red River or a hotdish shortage during wedding season.

But Jenny realized she was not without sin. In fact, she was very aware of two that she had recently committed. The first was stealing the award-winning recipe for "Squash Surprise Hotdish" from her dying aunt's underwear drawer. The second was that Jenny, at age 42, had fallen madly in love with the Reverend Thomas Milano.

The Lutheran ministers she had known before had blonde hair and flat personalities. There were no ups or downs. Their lives seemed to be pursued with a straightforwardness, like the green electronic line on the hospital heart monitor that indicates you are dead.

But the Rev. Milano, with his dark Mediterranean looks and body builder physique looked more like a gypsy, or even worse, a Catholic.

"He doesn't look like one of us," Jenny whispered to her husband during the Reverend's first Sunday morning sermon at Morningside Heights Lutheran.

Earl, a peaceful, round man who daydreamed of northern pike and new car batteries, merely nodded his head up and down like the bobbing Hawaiian hula dancer on the dashboard of his '92 pick-up.

"Yes, Dear," he responded, not hearing anything she or the minister said.

Earl had no way of knowing that during the Reverend's diatribe on love thy neighbor, Jenny had decided the words were a personal message to her and her alone. And there was no way to tell that, once again, Jenny had tumbled over the edge into what her latest shrink called maniac-depressive with obsessive-compulsive personality disorder. Earl just rolled his eyes at that. He knew Jenny was just plain crazy. Her doctor explained it was due to Jenny's growing up in an alcoholic and abusive home. Earl told the doctor "it's true her old man was the town drunk."

Jenny had, of course, endured obsessions before. Blessed nuisances she learned to call them in her bible-study group. True, she continually scrubbed her floors, but it yielded the cleanest house in town. And the ninety-seven autographs and five hundred candid snapshots of singer Wayne Newton were invaluable. She would have had an even larger collection if that nosy district attorney hadn't referred to her hobby as stalking.

She gazed up at the Reverend and thought, "Look at his beautiful, beautiful eyes. Why, if you put those eyes in a pickling jar and set the jar on the top shelf in the pantry, they would still, somehow, manage to show you the world."

And then there was his smile, or rather half smile, like a bashful boy who had just encountered his first love.

And the body - oh Christ! She envisioned him working out with weights at the YMCA. She fantasized him jogging on country roads in tight, black shiny shorts that clung to his massive, sweating thighs.

It should be against church law for a minister to exercise, Jenny decided. It can only lead to trouble, even if he is married.

And married he was. Jenny could tell that his wife was a Lutheran from birth. She had the same margarine-colored hair as Jenny, as well as skin the color of skim milk. But the minister's wife had one major flaw. She was horribly overweight, by at least twenty pounds.

Jenny looked down at her own size four body. She was fortunate to have a high metabolism as well as a three-pack-a-day cigarette habit. One thing Jenny would never do was gain weight. Last month, when her psychiatrist put her on a higher dose of medication, she gained two pounds in a week. She immediately stopped taking the prescription. She didn't bother to let her doctor know.

Besides, she was right in eliminating the pills. Not only did she lose the excess poundage she had gained but she found she loved being drug-free.

Anyways, Jenny knew she didn't have a problem. She was merely too highly evolved and complex for most people to understand. She was like those wordy math problems that asked if a train was traveling at sixty miles an hour and twelve people were on board and they were going to a family reunion and there were four or five conductors - how many passengers would be in the dining car?

Jenny comforted herself knowing that someday, soon, everyone would know just how right she had been all along about everything. Especially about becoming the new minister's wife.

Jenny Milano, she repeated to herself over and over during the offertory. Jenny Milano. It sounded like a movie star's name. Earl didn't even notice, that like a little girl with a crush on her teacher, Jenny had written over and over on the Sunday bulletin, "Mrs. Jenny Milano."

Fortunately for Jenny, there were only two minor obstacles to overcome before she could claim her fate - the Reverend's current wife and Earl.

Later, on that glorious and sunny Sunday afternoon, Jenny sat in her kitchen reorganizing her Woman's Day Planner. She was fully aware that accomplished people not only carried Day Planners but used them. Hers was a dark brown vinyl one from WalMart. It included a daily calendar, calorie chart, food journal, attitude of gratitude page, a place for names and addresses, a sheet describing the difference between meters and ounces, and a To Do section that was categorized into day, month and year. Jenny, who excelled in outlining in middle school, immediately began to formulate her goals: 1) make the Reverend fall in love with her; or 2) get Earl and the Mrs. out of the way by divorce, death or a combination of both.

Jenny chose to combine. But first things first. She needed to make the Reverend fall in love with her. That would be easy enough. She believed she could make any man fall in love with her, just like she had Earl.

All you needed to know was a man's deepest

fantasies and then fulfill them, at least until the license was signed. With Earl, it had been as easy as stealing candy from an anorexic. They had met on a blind date. A co-worker of Jenny's had set them up. Jenny knew it was meant to be a joke but she could never figure out on whom.

Earl was, after all, too common for her. As a child, lying in bed, trying to fall asleep while her parents fought, Jenny daydreamed of marrying either Prince Charles or John F. Kennedy, Jr. Earl was neither. His personality was as interesting as a sofa pillow. He didn't say more than two words during the entire evening.

That, however, turned out to be a good thing. His silence allowed Jenny to chatter away. And since Earl didn't tell her to shut up like the others had, she knew he was mad about her.

When Earl didn't return her numerous calls the next morning, or send the bouquet of daisies that she had hinted for, Jenny realized she had to, as usual, take matters into her own hands.

As Earl stocked shelves at the Piggly Wiggly, Jenny let herself into his home. (Fortunately Earl had mentioned that he liked living in a place like Morningside Heights because it meant he never had to lock his doors.) Jenny assumed correctly that Earl was a 28-year-old virgin and, like most unful-filled men, had a strong sex drive. The proof was in his 42" waist. Powdered donuts double as a sexual pacifier.

Jenny crept through his house looking for evidence of what Earl wanted in a woman. Once she reached his bedroom, it was as obvious as he was.

Above the bed was a poster of Farrah Fawcett. Her long blond and blow-dried hair gleamed like a shrine over Earl's twin bed.

By six that evening, Jenny sauntered into the Piggly Wiggly, wearing a tight leather mini-skirt and glitter tube top that made her cleavage jump out like the pink grapefruit that were on sale for forty-nine cents each. She had come straight from Hilda's Hairitage Beauty Salon where Hilda had bleached, curled, added extensions, and sprayed Jenny's bangs up and as stiff as a rooster's comb.

Jenny was, in her own way, a walking Farrah poster.

As soon as Earl saw her walking down the aisle, he dropped the case of prune juice he was holding. They were married within the month.

It would however, be a bit more difficult to trap the Reverend. For one thing, a parsonage filled with kids is harder to break into then a bachelor's bungalow. Of course, there was always the chance that once the Reverend knew Jenny, he would simply fall in love with her. Stranger things have happened.

"Whadda'ya doing going to the church on a Monday morning?" Earl asked, as Jenny pick up her car keys.

"I am the new volunteer driver for Meals on Wheels."

"You don't care about old people."

"I do now," Jenny said, lighting up a Camel cigarette.

"That the uniform for drivers?" Earl asked

skeptically.

"Of course not," Jenny answered, decked out in a pair of royal blue workout tights and a striped red and white leotard. "I thought I'd work out at my club on the way home."

"You don't have a club."

"You don't know everything about me, Earl Borgson," Jenny said storming out of the house.

"I know too much about you," Earl mumbled as he clicked on a rerun of Gomer Pyle.

After her workout and noticing that the Reverend was not at the club as she had fantasized, she drove to the church where 75 seniors were scheduled to eat a government sponsored lunch. Through the church's outreach program, 33 other meals were delivered to senior homes. Jenny had wanted to work next to the Reverend in the food line serving meals. He insisted, however, that she deliver them instead.

Jenny was about to say no way in hell was she going into "urine and cat-filled houses" but decided against it. If she was going to be a minister's wife, she'd have to learn to endure such crap.

"It'll be my burden to bear," Jenny stated as she lifted the basket filled with box lunches. She could tell by the Reverend's startled expression that he was surprised she knew such Bible verses.

By the third day, eight of the ten seniors on Jenny's list had refused to accept meals from a cursing, belligerent, chain-smoking driver. Jenny was now promoted to the food line. Another sign, she noted in her diary that night. The Reverend would come to lean on her, trust in her, and then turn to her when his wife died.

Life is good, Jenny noted in her "Don't Sweat The Small Stuff" diary. She filled the rest of the page with little, round, smiley faces.

The next morning, Jenny patiently waited at the front door of the public library. As soon as the doors were opened she rushed to the mystery writer's reference section. As usual it was the best resource to plan a crime.

She had decided to do away with the minister's wife first. She checked out *"The Fine Art of Murder,"* *"Deadly Doses: A Writer's Guide to Poison,"* and seven Sue Grafton books for inspiration.

Once at home, Jenny discovered that the possibilities for death were endless. Poison, of course, being the murder du jour for most women. Casseroles that killed were commonplace. There were knives, guns, smotherings, cliff pushings, hangings and drownings.

That caught her eye. Death by drowning. It had a nice ring to it.

After a few hours of reading, Jenny placed the books on the top shelf in her store room. She was giddy with excitement and energy. In fact, she had so much energy that she hadn't needed to sleep for days (another reason not to take medicine). Even Earl said she seemed a little manic when he caught her weeding the neighbor's garden. But without her medicine she accomplished so much more. After the murder she even planned to wallpaper the basement.

But first she needed to put all of her energies into a pool party.

For the first time she felt happy that Earl had bought that stupid, cheap, used backyard pool. It was the above ground kind, four feet deep and sixteen feet in circumference. Her flabby husband would spend hot summer afternoons floating on a lime green foam lounge chair while sipping a beer and listening to the radio talk show "Garage Logic" on his Sony Walkman. Jenny would circle the outside of the pool in anger, furious he hadn't bought the in-ground pool she had begged for.

But now, for the first time, it was a blessing. Who could resist an invitation to a pool party? Certainly not the minister's wife. Besides, she was new in town and was surely desperate for friends. Jenny knew how hard that could be on a person.

She mailed the invitations that evening. She sent thirty-four in all. Of course, most of the people she invited weren't her friends, just names from the church directory. But the invitation was so cute that she knew at least some of them would come. And except for the minister's wife, every invitation said to arrive at 1:00 p.m. For Mrs. Milano, it was noon sharp!

The one hour between the minister's wife's arrival and the rest of the guests provided the minister's wife enough time to stuff herself. Then Jenny and she would head to the pool where Jenny would help the current Mrs. Milano to drown.

Jenny knew the minister's wife could not turn down any food that was offered to her. All Jenny had to do was tempt the woman with her buttery hotdish made with summer squash and sedatives and then head straight to the pool for a dip, where

Jenny would gladly hold Mrs. Milano's head under water.

Later she would tell the police, "I told my dear friend to wait an hour after eating such an enormous meal but she wouldn't listen. I suppose she wanted to work off the calories, the poor, dead thing."

When Mrs. Milano called on Friday with her RSVP, Jenny danced a jig of happiness in the kitchen. Earl just looked at her and went to the family room and popped in a copy of "Charlie's Angels" on the VCR.

The party was scheduled for Saturday afternoon when Earl would be at work. Jenny drove to Sam's Club that morning and spent more than she should have on fancy, frozen stuffed mushroom appetizers and mini-chocolate creme puffs. She set them out, along with veggie trays, chips, macaroni salads, roasts, a turkey, chickens, onion dips, Cheetos, and five dozen frosted cupcakes. She had been cooking all week. There was enough food for fifty people, even though only four had responded to the invitation.

Jenny had just turned on the radio for peppy background music when the doorbell rang. She ran to answer it. In her haste to set up the party she hadn't noticed that she had forgotten to get out of her pajamas. She giggled when she realized she had worn them to Sam's Club that morning.

It just proved to her that people didn't care about anyone anymore. They used to tell you when your slip was showing; now they don't even tell you when you're out in your undies.

"Come in, come in," Jenny said so fast that Mrs. Milano had to ask her to repeat what she said.

Jenny noticed that the Mrs. was acting weird, kind of nervous-like, looking around the room as if she expected the others to already be there.

"Well, the early bird gets the worm," Jenny laughed, placing her hands on the minister's wife's shoulders and pushing her towards the buffet table.

"Oh, my," Mrs. Milano said, looking at the enormous gastronomical spread before her. "How many are you expecting?"

"That's for me to know and you to find out. Hey, is your bathing suit under your clothes? The pool's right outside the window," Jenny said pointing towards it.

"It's in my bag," Mrs. Milano said as she held up a canvas tote bag and glanced out at the backyard.

"Do you want to change now or after you eat?" Jenny asked impatiently.

"Afterwards, I suppose." Mrs. Milano answered. "I'm afraid I'm not that hungry."

"Yeah, right," Jenny laughed as she filled a plate with her squash surprise and handed it to Mrs. Milano.

Mrs. Milano tried small talk at first but Jenny would have none of it. She had questions that needed to be answered before it was too late.

What was the Reverend's favorite food? When was his birthday? Did he mind the fact that his wife was so fat? Of course, Jenny added that there was nothing personal intended in that question.

Mrs. Milano ate only one heaping tablespoon of the squash dish before she asked what was in it.

"You know women and hotdish," Jenny laughed. "The ingredients are always a secret. But I will tell you there is summer squash, creamed butter, toasted almonds and a special spice."

Mrs. Milano looked hard and long at the dish in front of her and then lifted her head and smiled.

"God bless you, Jenny," Mrs. Milano said quietly. "This dish is so wonderful that I am taking it into the bathroom while I change into my bathing suit. I can't stop eating it!"

"Of course, of course," Jenny chuckled, leading her to the bathroom. "And there's always seconds when you come out."

Jenny heard the bathroom lock click. Typical, prudish minister's wife, Jenny thought and vowed never to be that way herself.

Jenny waited patiently in the kitchen, looking out at the pool every once in a while, and smiling as she inhaled deeply on one cigarette after another. She hoped the Reverend wouldn't ask her to give up smoking. But perhaps she could do it for him. A minister's wife had to set a good example, after all.

It took only ten minutes for Earl, Reverend Milano and the police to arrive. Jenny learned later, after being reinstated on her medicine, that Mrs. Milano had called from her cellular phone while in the bathroom.

Jenny also learned that Mrs. Milano thought something odd was going on when Jenny opened the door in her pajamas and lipstick was streaked across her face, like she had missed noticing where her mouth was. Jenny also learned that she reeked from three days of not bathing and that Earl had emptied the pool the day before. She hadn't even noticed that, although Mrs. Milano had.

When the minister's wife called the Reverend for help, he immediately drove to the Piggly Wiggly. He and Earl jumped in their cars and called the police on the way.

Later, tranquil and functioning reasonably well, Jenny decided she was right to do what she did. The Minister and his wife seemed closer. Trauma does that to a couple. And of course Earl wanted to move once again. And that meant she and Earl would get to leave that stupid cheap pool behind. Who knew what could happen next? Maybe they'd even find a new town, and a new house with an in-ground pool, and a new minister and his wife.

The Maltese Tater Tot

It was a crazy kind of morning. Too many bill collectors, too many phone calls, and too few clients. It was the kind of frustrating a.m. where I wanted to be anywhere but where I was and do anything but what I was doing. You know the kind of day I'm talking about. The kind that usually leads to murder.

I was sitting at my desk, arms behind my head, smoking a Winston while gazing through the plate glass window that separated my assistant from me. I was staring at a shiny pair of legs. My secretary had returned from jogging and was still dressed in Spandex that fitted like an eighty-dollar pair of leather gloves.

I try to be discreet about my intense appreciation of the opposite sex. Not only is Dale the best secretary I've ever had, but I don't want him suing me for sexual harassment.

I'm Sarah Black of Strunk and Black Detective Agency. There's never been a Strunk. Early on I realized there was a deep prejudice against female investigators and if I wanted to earn a living I had to have a male partner, real or not.

At a garage sale I had found a discarded 8" x 10" photograph of a 70's kind of guy, complete with mint-green leisure suit, 14K gold-plated chains, and blow-dried hair. I hung the photo on my office wall. I glanced at the reference books on my desk and decided to name him Matt Strunk, as in Strunk and White of "The Elements of Style" fame.

I opened the agency in the warehouse district

of Minneapolis. My office is surrounded by seedy adult businesses and bad Chinese restaurants. The two always seem to go together. An hour after visiting either one you find yourself hungry for more.

In fact, I was just considering going to Chung Lou's for a bit of Chicken Almond Ding when Chuck Mittler arrived. I recognized his name immediately as being the founder of a chain of restaurants called Tater's.

He acted like most of my clients on their initial visit. His face was tight with anxiety. He looked cautiously around the office to make sure no one, except Dale and me, was there. The only difference between him and the others that walked in was that this one was drop-dead gorgeous. I put my desire for egg rolls on hold.

"How can I help you?" I asked as he sat down. I slid my cast iron "Ride the Ducks at Wisconsin Dells" ashtray towards him. He flicked an ash or two from his pricey cigar before he answered.

"It's my wife," he finally said, taking a long drag as he stared at Strunk's picture.

I waited to hear the typical spousal whine of "I'm afraid there's someone else," or "She's coming home late," or even worse, "I found underwear where there shouldn't have been underwear."

But he surprised me.

"My wife's emerald earrings were stolen last month from our house. Two weeks ago a diamond tennis bracelet was missing. And yesterday she announced that her 18K Gucci watch was gone."

"Have you contacted the police?" I asked

"No, and I won't."

"Why not?"

"Because I believe I know who's doing it."

"Who?" I asked, my ears perking up a bit.

"My wife."

Chuck spent the rest of the hour filling me in. His wife Christine was twenty years younger than he was. I guessed correctly that she was twenty-two. He said they met when she started working at one of his two dozen restaurants. It was love at first sight. He proposed within three weeks, they married within two days. That was eleven months ago.

"She was extraordinarily beautiful and viva-cious. I was surprised she was still on the market."

What market is that? I wanted to ask. Meat? Fruits and vegetables? Stock?

But instead I said, "Why do you think she's doing it?"

"That's what I haven't figured out. She has everything she needs. I deny her nothing. Her allowance is more than adequate."

I sat there looking at him, amazed at how good looking Neanderthals had become. There he was, a hugely successful businessman and yet a total moron when it came to women, wives in particular. He called her more-than-likely legal share of their money an "allowance." I wondered if he also made her stand in the corner when she was bad.

"I give her everything and she even insists on working when she doesn't have to. Christine says she likes working with her friends at the restau-rant. I let her do two banquets a week."

I wanted to scream. He "let" her work?

He thought of her as a kid. No wonder she was rebelling. I wanted to tell this jerk to go home and settle his own marriage problems but I checked out his Rolex and Armani suit. There was money to be had and there wasn't another man I'd rather take it from.

"I want to work with her. Can you arrange it?" I knew if I would find out anything about his wife, it would be away from him.

"No problem. You can even keep the tips you make," he laughed.

"I was planning to," I answered.

He agreed to have me work a banquet that evening. Christine would train me. He told me to wear a white shirt and black skirt. "Tight," he suggested with a hint of a smile.

I sent Dale to Dayton's to buy a straight skirt, size 12. I hinted that an elastic waist would be best. Dale came back with a size 16. It fit perfectly.

Meanwhile I had spent the time on the internet, finding out everything I could about Chuck Mittler and Tater's.

Mittler had made his fortune on a Minnesota phenomenon called hotdish. What would be merely an embarrassing assembly of leftovers drowning in canned cream soup in other parts of the world carried an almost sacred significance in Minnesota. Minnesotans are traditionally frugal and cold - temperature wise that is. Wives and mothers learn early on how to stretch a meal with canned soup, rice or potatoes, and a hint of meat. And if it were a special occasion, such as a 50th anniversary, the hotdish was topped with tiny taste bud explosives called Tater Tots.

Tater's Restaurant had taken Minnesota's up-home cooking to an extreme. Mittler toyed with the recipes, hired chatty servers, and designed colorful ceramic plates that were shaped like tractors. Minnesotans had flocked in to the restaurants and within a few years, dozens more opened in the Midwest.

He still managed the original Tater's in Fridley, a working class suburb north of the Twin Cities. I was scheduled to be there at 5:00 p.m.

"You're the new girl?" asked a six-foot voluptuous Nordic beauty as I walked into the restaurant. She moved her hips like a slow-moving caboose over the Rocky Mountains.

"You must be Christine," I said, pulling down my skirt that had ridden a few inches above my knees. I had forgotten to wear a slip. I was not use to wearing skirts. Trousers are my preferred apparel.

"You betcha. My husband said you've never worked in a restaurant before."

"No, but I have a lot of experience eating in them."

Christine's crystal-like giggles filled the room. I wasn't surprised that when it came to Christine, Chuck had taken a nose dive into idiotsville.

She led me into the kitchen and introduced me to the other "girls." There were Cindy, Ally and Mabel. They were all young, tattooed and had rings in their nostrils rather than on their fingers. Their tattoos ranged from a discrete rose on the ankle for Ally to a raging tiger on Mabel's forearm. They were your typical twenty-some-year-olds.

The chef, however, was not your average Joe. I guessed his weight to be around four hundred pounds. His face was clean shaven and resembled the moon. I could almost see a man in it. To add insult to his genetic injury, of course he was called Tiny.

The assistant cook was another matter. He had to weigh two hundred pounds with one hundred ninety of that being muscle. His name was Jordan. His long black hair was tied back into a ponytail. He, too, was tattooed and highly bejeweled. A small gold chain ran from his nostril to his lip, and each earlobe had five piercings with accompanying attachments. Three metal studs were imbedded above each eyebrow. He would never make it through a security gate at the airport without setting off an alarm.

Christine chatted and laughed with everyone. Jordan couldn't keep his eyes off her. Tiny was too busy to do anything but cook, but I could tell he was paying close attention to everything she said.

Each of them could have considered Christine their boss but I could tell they didn't. The atmosphere was jovial until Chuck walked in and it immediately froze.

Chuck snapped his fingers in the air three times. "Come on, ladies, get a move on."

As he left the room, Cindy whispered "Jerk" to Mabel. It was loud enough for everyone to hear, including Christine, who nodded her head in agreement.

The banquet party started to arrive. It was the Fridley's Curling Club Awards Dinner. Curling is an ancient sport that is still popular in Minnesota. Eons ago men spent afternoons using broomsticks to push large round stones across frozen lakes. Television had not yet been invented.

The menu began with an iceberg lettuce salad drenched in thousand island dressing. Baskets of white buns and pats of butter sat next to each tractor plate. The entrees were served family style in huge bowls that resided in the middle of the table. The main dishes were "Old Fashioned Tater Surprise" or the trendier "Cajun Shrimp Hotdish". Dessert was a selection of nut bars and miniature lime green Jello jigglers shaped like walleye.

I worked harder than I had in years. I've never known anyone to drink as much coffee as Minnesotans do. We filled each cup at least five times. In the kitchen the chefs stirred, cooked, and swore at us every chance they got. Christine said not to mind the yelling, that it was a chef's nature to do so. By the time the last customer left, my crisp white blouse was soaked in sweat. Even Christine was mopping her forehead. Her husband occasionally stared through the door just to make sure everything was going smoothly.

Within forty minutes the tables were cleared and the condiments put away. My pockets were filled with cash. To celebrate I stood in the back alley with my fellow employees smoking a much needed cigarette.

"That was a rough one," Mabel said, kicking a

piece of paper out of her way.

"They were nice though," Christine said. I noticed that she always tried to look at the bright side of things. I couldn't see her as a crook but then I've been fooled before.

"They were better than soccer moms," Ally noted.

"Anyone's better than a soccer mom," Jordan replied. I looked at his face that had more hardware than Home Depot. I gave myself two to one odds his own mother was a rich soccer mom. Jordan seemed very out of place. Even with all of his body decorations it was easier to see him with a tennis racket in his hand rather than a greasy spatula.

"We going out?" Tiny asked Christine. I gathered he meant everyone.

"You betcha." Christine smiled warmly at him and then looked at me. "You wanna come with?"

"Where?" I asked.

Where turned out to be a bar called Slammers located in the downtown nightclub district. The average age at the club was 22. The average size slim to none. The other women and Jordan fit in well. Tiny and I stood out like roasted pigs at an animal rights convention.

"You like this place?" I asked Tiny as we squeezed into a back booth. By that time the rest of the crew were dancing to a live band called Decaying Squirrel Meat.

"Sure," he answered. I noticed Tiny didn't talk much. I also noticed something else. He and Christine were close friends. I couldn't tell if the vibes between them were sexual, however.

I had assumed that if Christine was dallying around with anyone it would be with the hunky Jordan who was at least her age. I was pretty sure he would welcome it. He had yet to take his eyes off of her. But then, who could?

But she seemed to prefer Tiny. He was at least fifteen years older than her and three times her size. But, when it comes to love all cats are gray in the dark.

I looked at the dance floor. Men were dancing with men, women with women. A lot of women or men were dancing alone. There was actually an occasional man and woman bumping together. It was certainly the twenty-first century. Inhibitions and social protocol were left back in the nineties.

"You wanna dance?" Mabel asked, returning to the table.

"Why not?" I said, knowing that absolutely no one I knew would be there anyway. My crowd of friends only did the Polka and even that reluctantly. By the time Mabel and I returned to the table Christine and Tiny were gone.

"Where'd they go?" I asked.

The others looked at each other. No one answered. Jordan sat there frowning, his fingers tapping heavily on the table. Finally, after I asked again, Ally responded. "Christine probably gave Tiny a ride home. He doesn't have a driver's license."

The five of us spent the rest of the evening drinking and talking. Whenever I could I turned the conversation around to the fact that I was surprised that Christine was married to Chuck, considering how old he was. Finally, after what seemed like hours of prodding, they responded.

"Too bad Chuck's not older," Robin cracked. "Then Christine could at least count on him dying soon."

"Next time she should try for a ninety year old," Jordan muttered.

"Do you think she married for money?" I casually asked, thinking I knew what their answer would be. I didn't.

"Worse," Ally answered quickly. "She married for love."

Even though each of them hated Mittler, it seemed Christine loved him. He was a stern, uncompromising employer. If anyone broke any of his rules, no matter what the reason, they were terminated. And although he couldn't stop it, he didn't like his staff fraternizing with each other.

"The thing I don't like about Mittler," Ally continued, "is that he's so paranoid about everything. For example, he refuses to hire anyone who's related to another employee. I think that sucks."

"Yet he goes and marries an employee. If that's not unfair, I don't know what is," Jordan said. "Aren't you related if you're married?"

"Technically, yes," I told him. "Don't you guys have a union?"

I never knew I could be so funny. They laughed for at least three minutes.

I was still wound up by the time I got back to my apartment at 1:30 a.m. I decided to do what a lot of single women do, alone, late at night. I wasn't even embarrassed about it. I quietly slid the video into the VCR and sat back and waited for the fun to begin.

Forget Tom Cruise, Kevin Costner or Harrison Ford. No one is sexier than Humphrey Bogart as Sam Spade in "The Maltese Falcon."

Bogie's the reason I became a P.I. He's the epitome of coolness. He's a cynical realist yet still vulnerable to a pretty face. He sees life in black and white and good or bad. He knows he has faults, lots of them. He tries to do the right thing, even though he often doesn't want to.

And when he falls in love it's always at a safe, comfortable distance. Early on in life I decided that Sam Spade and I had a lot in common. I also decided that being a private investigator sounded more interesting than typing for a living.

As soon as the final movie credits rolled I fell asleep on the couch. It was ten o'clock before I woke up and headed to the office.

Dale had a cup of French Roast waiting for me. He also had a fax from Mittler. I glanced at it as I sat at my desk and turned on the computer. I was scheduled to meet Christine for a late lunch. I had convinced her I knew this really "cool" place on the river front. Being "cool" is very important for anyone under thirty. But first I had to start on the dirty work.

Mittler had faxed me the social security numbers and names of all of his employees. Three decades ago I'd be wearing out good shoe leather trying to get the info I needed. But it was the new millennium and all I had to do was jump on the internet.

Much of my detective work is done there. I can track records ranging from births, obituaries, alumni listings, social security info, newspaper records, and credit histories.

I charge a client $250 to find a runaway or deadbeat dad. The internet company I use to locate the sucker charges me a mere fifty bucks. Not a bad profit.

But today I wasn't looking for anyone. I was looking for a connection - anything that might tie Christine to another employee. If she was stealing from her husband, I was pretty sure it was connected to the staff at Tater's.

It took me only an hour to find out what I needed to know. That gave me two hours to stew it over before I met Christine.

She was already waiting for me, seated on the restaurant's sidewalk patio. On the table in front of her were a half dozen drinks sent from the various wolf hounds at the bar. Christine hadn't touched any of them. She was sipping a Perrier and reading a Danielle Steel novel when I arrived. I decided to sit with her anyway.

"Hi, ya," she smiled up at me. "You were right. This place is cool."

"The appetizers are great," I told her. Last night I noticed her appetite was enormous. Yet, there wasn't an ounce of fat on her body. I could have hated her just for that but I didn't. I liked her instead.

I ordered a sampler plate of deep-fried onion blossoms, fried mushrooms, jo-jo potatoes and buffalo wings. We sat there with our Diet Cokes while dipping thousands of calories into a spicy ketchup.

"I hear you're a newlywed," I said as I grabbed my fourth wing.

"Not hardly," she laughed. "It's been almost a year."

"I don't mean to get personal, but isn't he a bit gruff?"

"Oh, he's just like that at work. He's a crappy boss but a big teddy bear of a husband."

"Like Tiny was?" I asked.

I never saw anyone actually turn a shade of green before. I was hoping it wasn't the wings.

"How did you...?"

"Know? One of your friends drank a little too much last night. You know what they say, loose lips..."

Christine just sat there, first looking betrayed and then furious. Her sweet demeanor had quickly dissolved.

"Damn, Ally," she mumbled out loud.

I, of course, had not heard a thing. But, when people have secrets they shouldn't tell, they normally tell at least one person. And it's usually the person with the biggest mouth.

"See Chuck still doesn't know," she said quietly. "I've been meaning to tell him but the longer I wait, the more awkward it becomes."

"Why didn't you tell him in the first place?"

"Well, he never asked if I'd been married before. And it all happened so quickly. One day we were here and the next day at the Little Chapel of the

West in Las Vegas. Besides, I didn't want Tiny to get fired. He needs the money too badly."

"You think Chuck would have fired him?

"Chuck has a strict policy against hiring relatives. He's dead set against it. Tiny got me the job in the first place. Besides, I wasn't married to Tiny that long. I didn't think it was that big of a deal."

Somehow I knew she wasn't lying.

"How long were you married?" I asked, although my time on the internet and a little bit of illegal hacking had already give me my answer. I just wanted to see how honest she was.

"A couple of months. We realized quickly it was a mistake."

"Was this before Tiny went to prison?"

"You know about that too? Gosh, just how much did Ally drink?"

I didn't respond. It wasn't Ally that told me. Police records proved that the cooking school Tiny attended was Stillwater State Prison.

A newspaper report stated that Tiny had loved the slots at Mystic Lake Casino. Unfortunately, they didn't love him back. He embezzled $65,000.00 from Twin City Federal before he was caught.

"Did she tell you I met him at a G.A. and GamAnon inter-group rally?" Christine asked.

"Of course," I lied. Fortunately I knew what she meant, being a bit compulsive myself. G.A. referred to Gamblers Anonymous and GamAnon was the program for those affected by compulsive gamblers in their lives.

"My brother was a gambler," Christine said

sadly. "He killed himself after spending his mort-gage payments on lottery scratch-offs. Tiny's life reminds me of him."

"But the relationship between the two of you didn't take?"

"No, it didn't. Tiny's a good guy and all - but hey, he wasn't that crazy about me. He prefers heavier women."

Birds of a bigger feather, I thought.

"Is Tiny back to gambling?" I asked.

"God no. He's been clean for two years. He's the best speaker G.A. has."

I was back to square one. If Tiny was following a rigid twelve-step program based on honesty, he wouldn't be able to justify stealing. And I still couldn't see Christine as a thief. I wondered si-lently why her husband did. I was scheduled to work another banquet that evening. If I didn't find anything out by then, I'd have to tell Chuck I'd come up empty handed. He'd have to pay me more money or set me free. However, when I looked across the street I saw a glimmer of a clue drinking a large espresso.

Christine left and I headed back to my office. I called Chuck to tell him my plan. I asked him not to tell Christine. I'd do so later. I jumped on the internet and made a few phone calls. I was con-vinced I knew who the thief was but I needed Christine's help to prove it. I waited for her in the parking lot that evening. She agreed to help.

The banquet party that evening was for Catho-lics Against Drug Abuse. I chuckled at the name, wondering where the Catholics "For" Drug Abuse were holding their banquet. The menu was "Tater's Three Cheese Hotdish" along with the overwhelming artery-clogging "Hot Buttered Paprika Chicken with Creamed Rice Hotdish."

"Can't you damn people move any faster?" Tiny yelled, sweat dripping off his forehead. Fortunately he caught it before it hit the food.

"Get screwed," Cindy snipped back.

We were crazy busy - enough so that I was afraid Christine would forget to do what I had asked her to do. But she didn't. In the kitchen in the middle of it all, plates moving, cups flying, bowls being dropped, she turned and announced "this scarf is driving me nuts."

She undid the red silk scarf that held her hair back and laid it on a counter. She didn't explain why a scarf could drive her nuts. No one would care except for the one person who cared too much.

Tiny was at the back burner and the rest of us, Christine included, hustled back into the banquet hall. I turned and watched through the small window of the door to the kitchen as Jordan grabbed the scarf. He turned around to see if Tiny was looking and, realizing he wasn't, placed the scarf over his face. He inhaled deeply. To him it was the Garden of Eden. He turned and hid the scarf inside a Tater's menu and then rubbed the menu over and over. He acted as if it was the Maltese Falcon, hiding the world's most precious jewels.

I was convinced Jordan had taken the other items only because they were Christine's. They could have been discarded chewing gum wrappers and he would have worshipped them as much. And

I was pretty sure that if I asked him, he would defend his actions as "being in love." The term stalking meant nothing to him. And according to the police records I had located, he had been "in love" with many women before.

We waited until the end of the shift to approach him. By that time the only employees left were Chuck, Christine and me. We asked everyone else to leave.

Chuck stood next to the counter. I could tell he was controlling his rage. Chuck had had no idea that Jordan was obsessed with his wife. When I had told him what I suspected, he had channeled his enormous guilt about suspecting his wife into fury towards Jordan.

He was containing himself well but I made sure he stayed at the end of the counter, away from the kitchen knives.

"But why Jordan?" Christine asked, tears running down her face. "You knew I am in love with my husband."

"I can have you arrested for breaking into our home," Chuck stated.

Jordan rolled his eyes at Mittler. "The charges won't stick," Jordan told him. "They never do."

He was probably right. Jordan has a history of mental illness. A judge would take one look at Jordan's records and turn him over to his shrink.

I'd managed to discover that Jordan's history of stalking women included stealing their personal items. He never physically harmed the women and when he tired of his current obsession he mailed back the stolen goodies.

"Trust me, this time is different," Mittler told Jordan. "I can afford better lawyers than most."

Jordan just stared at him.

Mittler snapped his fingers in the air. The two policemen officers standing outside the kitchen door's window saw the cue to come in. Within minutes they were leaving the restaurant with Jordan handcuffed between them.

I wanted to tell Chuck his problems were over, but they weren't. It would be a long time before Christine would forgive him for not trusting her. She told him she would not even talk to him unless he received counseling. Christine stormed out of the restaurant. Tiny and the rest of the crew were waiting for her in the alley.

Mittler paid me but didn't bother to say thank you. He was too busy going through the yellow pages, looking for marriage counselors.

Hotdish Recipes

The following recipes are inspired by the zany characters in my tales or were contributed by the zanier characters in my life - my wonderful friends.

Spicy Fisherman's Hotdish

2 tablespoons butter
1 pound firm fish (cod) cut into small chunks
1 green pepper diced
1 red pepper diced
1 medium onion diced
1/4 teaspoon cayenne pepper
Liquid hot sauce
1/4 teaspoon red pepper flakes
2 cans cream of broccoli soup
1 can of milk
1/2 can water
1 cup long grain uncooked rice
Bread crumbs

Sauté cut-up fish in butter for three minutes. Remove fish. Sauté green and red peppers with onions. Set aside. Mix 2 cans of cream of broccoli soup with 1 can of milk and a 1/2 can of water. Add 1 cup rice. Add 1/4 teaspoon cayenne pepper, 1/4 teaspoon red pepper flakes, stir. Add liquid hot sauce to taste. Add cup of uncooked rice. Add fish chunks. Pour mixture into greased baking dish. Cover with bread crumbs. Bake for 35 minutes covered at 350 degrees. Remove cover. Bake for additional 30 minutes uncovered.

Company's Coming Potatoes

3 cups very thinly sliced red potatoes (skin off)
1 green pepper diced
1/2 onion diced
4 slices cooked crisp bacon
1 can cream of mushroom soup
1/2 can of Cheddar soup
1 and 1/2 can of milk
Fresh parsley

Sauté green peppers and onions. Add crumbled bacon. Stir well. In greased baking dish layer thinly sliced red potatoes. Mix cream of mushroom soup and Cheddar soup together with milk. Cover the potatoes, then layer the green peppers, onion and bacon mixture. Sprinkle fresh parsley on top. Bake for 35 minutes at 350 degrees. Remove cover, bake for additional 30 minutes.

Summer Squash Hotdish

2 large summer or yellow squash
1 can cream of chicken soup
1/2 cup sour cream
1/2 cup slivered almonds
Bread crumbs

Slice squash into 1/2 inch rounds. Steam until tender. Drain. Add cream of chicken soup, sour cream, and blanched almonds. Cover with bread crumbs. Bake for 10 minutes at 350 degrees.

Cajun Shrimp Hotdish

16 ounces frozen tails-off shrimp (small)
1 can cream of shrimp soup
1 can cream of mushroom soup
2 cups of milk
1 cup of long grain rice
1 red pepper diced small
1 teaspoon Cajun seasoning
Bread crumbs

Rinse frozen shrimp in cold water. In bowl mix together 1 can of cream of shrimp soup, 1 can of mushroom soup, 2 cups of milk. Add 1 teaspoon Cajun seasoning. Dice 1 red pepper, add to mixture. Add 1 cup rice and shrimp. Place bread crumbs on top. Cover and bake for 35 minutes at 350 degrees, then uncover and bake for additional 30 minutes.

Three Cheese Tater Hotdish

1 pound ground beef
One half green pepper
One half onion
1 can cream of potato soup
1 can cream of celery soup
Tater Tots (small bag)

1/3 cup shredded Mozzarella cheese
1/3 cup shredded Cheddar cheese
1/3 cup grated Parmesan cheese

Brown ground beef, green peppers, and onions together. Place in greased casserole dish. Add cream of potato soup, cream of celery soup. Mix well. Add Mozzarella, Cheddar, and Parmesan cheese. Cover with Tater Tots. Pour over beef mixture. Bake for 45 minutes at 350 degrees.

Old Fashioned Tater Surprise

1 pound hamburger
1 medium onion chopped
1/4 cup BBQ sauce
2 large rutabagas
1 can cream of mushroom soup
1 can of Cheddar soup
1 cup of milk
Tater Tots (small bag)

Brown hamburger with chopped onions and green peppers.
Mix in 1/4 cup BBQ sauce. Remove outer covering of rutabagas and slice into quarters. Then slice quarters into very thin
slices. Grease casserole dish. Layer hamburger mixture on
bottom. The lay rutabaga slices on top of mixture. Mix together cream of mushroom soup, Cheddar soup and milk.
Spread over rutabagas. Cover with layer of Tater Tots. Bake
for 35 minutes covered at 350 degrees. Remove cover. Bake
for additional 30 minutes uncovered.

Bubbly and bright, April Anderson always seem to be in a good mood. Maybe she's been eating her own cooking. Her recipe is a perfect example of a classic hotdish.

April Anderson's
Tater Tot Hotdish

Preheat oven to 350 degrees

1 1/2 pounds ground hamburger
1 can chicken gumbo soup
1/2 cup of grated cheese
1 can of cream of mushroom soup
Tater Tots (small bag)
1 can French fried onion

Brown and drain hamburger, place on bottom of 1 1/2 quart casserole dish, smooth over with spoon. Top with mixture of two soups, spread out evenly. Make a flat layer of Tater Tots on top. Sprinkle grated cheese on Tater Tots (spread around even). Bake covered for 45 minutes. Remove from oven. Sprinkle can of French fried onions on top. Bake uncovered for additional 15 minutes.

Barb Dibble is a traditional Nordic lass. She's tall, blonde, elegant, religious, and organized. All the things I'm not. I think that's why I like her so much.

Barb Dibble's
Five Star Hotdish

Preheat oven to 350 degrees

1 pound ground turkey
1 can cream of mushroom soup
1 can chicken with rice soup
1 soup can of water
1 cup white long grain rice uncooked

Brown ground turkey/drain if needed. Butter sides and bottom of covered casserole dish. In casserole dish mix together cream of mushroom soup, chicken with rice soup, one can of water. Add 1 cup uncooked long grain rice. Add cooked turkey. Cover and bake for 35 minutes. Uncover and bake for additional 30 minutes. Hamburger can be substituted for turkey.

Marjorie Myers Douglas is the author of "Eggs in the Coffee, Sheep in the Corn : My 17 years as a Farmwife" and "Barefoot on Crane Island: a Fond Reminiscence of Lake Minnetonka in the 1920s." She is also my mentor, social conscience, and hotdish interpreter.

Marjorie Myers Douglas
Chow Mein Noodle Hotdish

Preheat oven to 350 degrees

1 pound ground beef
1 chopped onion
1 cup of chopped celery
1/2 cup of uncooked rice
2 cups of water
1 can of cream of mushroom soup
1 can of chicken and rice soup
4 tablespoons Soy Sauce
2 tablespoons Worcestershire Sauce
Chow Mein noodles

Brown hamburger. Drain fat. Mix cream of mushroom soup, chicken and rice soup, and water. Add hamburger, uncooked rice, chopped onion, celery, Soy and Worcestershire sauce. Place in greased casserole dish. Bake for 1 1/2 hours. Serve over Chow Mein noodles.

Nora Feehan is a computer whiz and all-around swell gal. Though she lives in a Chicago suburb, she's a great hotdish cook. She has to be. Her husband Brent is originally from Eddyville, Iowa.

Nora Feehan's
Creamy Chili Hotdish

Preheat oven at 325 degrees

2 packages of macaroni and cheese
15 ounce can of no bean chili
8 ounce package of cream cheese softened
1 cup of shredded mild Cheddar cheese

Cook the macaroni and cheese, following package instructions. Mix the chili and cream cheese together and warm in a sauce-pan. After the macaroni and cheese is done, mix the chili cheese mixture with the macaroni and cheese. Place the mixture in a greased casserole dish and bake uncovered for 15 minutes or so until bubbly. Sprinkle Cheddar cheese on top and bake for additional 5 minutes or until cheese is melted.

Jean Fox teaches workshops on improving one's life. My knowing her has certainly improved mine. This recipe features the best part of a holiday dinner - stuffing!

Jean Fox's
Turkey & Stuffing Hotdish

Preheat oven to 350 degrees

6 cups leftover stuffing or 6 cups prepared stove top stuffing
3 cups leftover gravy OR 3 cups white sauce flavored with chicken bouillon
1 cup cooked peas
3 cups cut up turkey
Salt and pepper to taste

Create layers by placing half of stuffing mixture in bottom of greased 8 inch square baking dish, add turkey, peas, 1 cup of gravy, and rest of stuffing. Pour remaining gravy over all. Bake for 30 minutes.

Donna Kopitzke is everything that makes Wisconsin great. She's super-friendly, a devoted Green Bay Packers' fan, and an admitted cheese lover. She's also one of the best cooks I know.

Donna Kopitzke's
Hotdish Fishdish

Preheat oven to 375 degrees

1 1/2 pounds of cod
1 pint of whipping cream
1/2 cup chopped onions
5 tablespoons butter
I cup broccoli florets
1 cup grated sharp Cheddar cheese
1 1/2 cup dried bread crumbs
1 teaspoon fresh dill
1/2 teaspoon salt
1/4 teaspoon pepper

Melt butter in large skillet and sauté onions till almost clear. Add 1 cup broccoli florets. Add salt and pepper. Mix well; turn off heat and add cheese. Stir thoroughly. Place fish into a 9 x 9 cake pan. Pour whipping cream over fish. Spread bread crumb mixture evenly over top of fish. Sprinkle fresh dill. Bake in oven for 30-45 minutes or until fish is flaky white. Good hot or cold.

Comedian Codey Livingood is my favorite road partner. He's amazingly funny, very often brilliant, and as you can see from his original recipe, a bit loony as well.

Codey Livingood's
SPAM Parmesan

1 can of SPAM luncheon meat
1 can of cream of mushroom soup
1/2 cup whole milk
1/3 cup freshly grated Parmesan cheese
1/2 teaspoon garlic powder
8 ounce package of fettucini noodles

Dice SPAM into small pieces and heat in skillet at low heat. Pour cream of mushroom soup over SPAM. Add milk. Sprinkle Parmesan cheese and garlic powder over mixture and simmer for 5 minutes. Prepare noodles per package directions. Mix noodles with sauce and serve.

Marit Livingood is the only highly creative person I know whose house and closets are spotless. Her recipes are like she is - fun, tasteful, and of course, efficient.

Marit Livingood's
Lutheran Soul Food
(Tuna Noodle Hotdish)

Preheat oven 425 degrees

1 1/2 cups wavy egg noodles
1 can cream of mushroom soup
1/2 cup canned evaporated milk
7 ounce can of tuna drained
Half an onion chopped
1 cup grated American cheese (Marit prefers sliced Velveeta)
1/2 cup broken potato chips

Boil noodles as per package directions and drain. Combine with remaining ingredients and pour into 1 1/2 quart baking dish, topping with 1/2 cup broken potato chips. Bake uncovered for 15 minutes.

Mary Rogers may be an earnest and noble professor, but she is a comedian's dream audience. She cracks up at everything - including when I asked her for her favorite hotdish recipe.

Mary Rogers'
North Dakota Hotdish

Preheat oven to 350 degrees

1 pound ground beef
1 medium onion
1 or 2 cans sliced potatoes (4 c sliced)
1 can whole kernel corn
1 teaspoon salt
1 teaspoon pepper
1/4 cup sliced pimentos
1 can cream of mushroom soup
1 can milk

Brown ground beef and onions. Add salt and pepper. Pour off drippings. Place mixture into one layer in 13 x 9 baking pan. Layer potatoes on top of ground beef mixture. In small bowl combine corn, pimentos, soup and milk. Mix thoroughly and layer on top. Bake for 1 1/2 hours.

Comedian Sharon Rush always makes me laugh. She claims she's "Minnesota nice with a pinch of nastiness for spice." Even her hotdish makes me smile.

Sharon Rush's
Cheap & Easy Cabbage Hotdish
(High fiber - Low class)

High Brow Version

One pound of ground round
Three cups of shredded cabbage (1 small to medium cabbage)
1 can Campbell's Tomato Soup

Lower Brow Version

One pound cheap hamburger
Three cups shredded cabbage
1 can generic tomato soup

Brown the meat, drain fat (or not). Salt and pepper to taste. Layer shredded cabbage on bottom of casserole. Top cabbage with cooked meat. Spread soup over the top. Bake for one hour at 350 degrees.

Sandy Thomas is a wonderful actor, superb director and mom extraordinaire. However a great cook she's not, according to her. This is one of five simple recipes that she does make.

Sandy Thomas'
If I can do it - You can do it Hotdish

Preheat oven to 350 degrees

1 package of frozen chopped spinach
1 jar 32 oz spaghetti sauce
1 cup of water
1 egg
1 carton 16 ounces Ricotta cheese
2 packages (8 ounces) shredded Mozzarella cheese
1 package uncooked manicotti shells
1 goblet of red wine
Freshly grated Parmesan Cheese

Cook spinach. Drain and squeeze dry, set aside. Place one cup of the spaghetti sauce in greased baking dish. Stir in water and 1/4 goblet of wine. In a medium bowl beat the egg, ricotta cheese, two cups mozzarella and spinach until blended. Fill the shells with the mixture and arrange in baking dish. Spoon the sauce over the shells, cover tightly with foil. Drink the remaining goblet of wine while waiting for dish to cook. Bake for 1 1/4 hours, remove the foil and sprinkle with remaining Mozzarella. Bake for 3-5 minutes until melted. Top with freshly grated Parmesan cheese.

Zola Thompson is the first friend I made in Minnesota. She alone was worth the move. Her hotdish recipe is the one I take to parties. It always received rave reviews.

Zola Thompson's
Chicken & Wild Rice

Preheat oven to 325 degrees

3 - 4 pounds chicken breasts cut up
1 can of cream of mushroom soup
1 cup water
1/2 can of milk
1 package of dry onion soup mix
1 Box Uncle Ben's' Wild Rice Mix
1 seasoning packet from inside of Uncle Ben's Wild Rice Box

Sprinkle dry onion soup mix in bottom of ungreased 9 x 13 pan. Spread Uncles Ben's Rice over the dry soup. Spread the uncooked chicken pieces over the rice. Mix water and milk together. Pour the mixture over the chicken and rice. Sprinkle the Uncle Ben's seasoning package over the top. Bake 2 hours uncovered. Watch carefully and add water or milk if necessary.

About The Author

Pat Dennis is an award-winning author and comedian. Her fiction has been published in such magazines as *Woman's World* and *Minnesota Monthly*. She won first place in the SASE and Borders Short Fiction Contest for her short story "Bronte Rides The Bingo Bus." Her comedy performances include Dudley Riggs' *"What's So Funny About Being Female?"* and *"Minnesota's Funniest Women"* at Knuckleheads Comedy Club in The Mall of America. Pat is in high demand for national conventions, corporate events, employee parties, clubs, civic organizations and women's health expos.

If you are interested in booking Pat Dennis call (612) 869-7979 or write Comedy by Pat Dennis, P.O. Box 23058, Richfield, MN 55423.